Naveed

TITLES IN THIS SERIES

THROUGH MY EYES
series editor Lyn White

Naveed

JOHN HEFFERNAN

ALLEN&UNWIN

SYDNEY·MELBOURNE·AUCKLAND·LONDON

Australian Government

Australia Council
for the Arts

This project has been assisted by the Australian Government through the Australia Council, its arts funding and advisory body.

A portion of the proceeds (up to $5000) from sales of this series will be donated to UNICEF. UNICEF works in over 190 countries, including those in which books in this series are set, to promote and protect the rights of children. www.unicef.org.au

First published in 2014

Text © John Heffernan 2014
Series concept © series creator and series editor Lyn White 2014

Allen & Unwin
83 Alexander Street
Crows Nest NSW 2065
Australia
Phone: (61 2) 8425 0100
Email: info@allenandunwin.com
Web: www.allenandunwin.com

A Cataloguing-in-Publication entry is available from the National Library of Australia – www.trove.nla.gov.au

ISBN 978 1 74331 248 3

Teaching and learning guide available from www.allenandunwin.com

Cover and text design by Bruno Herfst & Vincent Agostino
Set in 11pt Plantin by Midland Typesetters, Australia
Cover photos: portrait of young boy by David Sacks/Getty Images, helicopter by Ton Koene/Getty Images
Map of Afghanistan by Guy Holt
This book was printed in March 2015 at Griffin Press, 168 Cross Keys Road, Salisbury South SA 5106.
www.griffinpress.com.au

15 14 13 12 11 10 9 8 7

To my three girls

By the time I become a big man I think Afghanistan will be peaceful and rebuilt. And it will not be destroyed again. The children will not allow it.
BULTAN, AGE 9

One child, one teacher, one book, one pen can change the world.
MALALA YOUSAFZAI

If it's the truth you want, ask a child.
AFGHAN SAYING

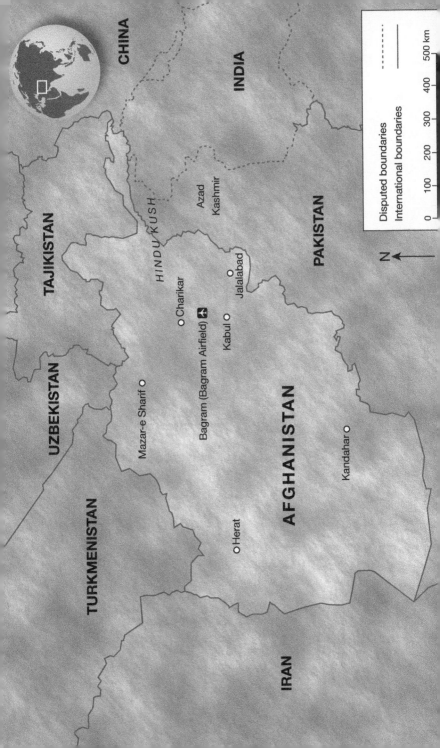

Chapter 1

The explosion jolts him awake. He sits up, gasping for air, heart thumping.

Was the blast real? Perhaps it had only happened in his head, a bad dream. He'd had plenty of those, nightmares real as real. *Demons of the dark*, his father called them.

Push them away. They'll only poison your thoughts. Seek the light and they can't hurt you.

The boy peers hard into the tiny room where he lives with his mother and sister. He listens intently. But the room gives nothing back. Its mud walls hunch over him. The two windows, holes patched with plastic bags, look down like a dead man's eyes. The blanket covering the low doorway to the outside shifts in the morning breeze: a mouth that might speak but only sighs. He catches a whiff of its stale breath, a mix of smells he knows well – garbage, diesel, sewage, dust. He grimaces. But almost immediately his father's words are there again.

1

In every darkness there is light, Naveed. Never forget that. Always look for the light.

'Yes, Padar,' he whispers into the pre-dawn greyness that fills the room. 'I will.'

He means it. He will never forget anything his father said. Never. And he does always seek the light, or at least tries his hardest to do so.

'It's just not that easy, Padar. Without you here the darkness seems so great.'

The darker it gets, the harder you must seek. Padar always had an answer, always a reason to see good, even when it seemed to be nowhere in sight. *The world lives on hope.*

'You are right, Padar.'

Of course, there is much to thank Allah for, Naveed has to admit as he looks around the room they moved into barely a fortnight ago. It might be tiny and cramped, with a wide crack down one wall and a ceiling in need of repair, but it is a thousand times better than the tent they lived in for almost two years after Padar died. Perishingly cold in winter, unbearably hot and filled with dust in summer, its threadbare canvas was often torn or flattened by the strong winds that blew across the plains from the Hindu Kush.

The room is heaven by comparison – a solid roof over their heads, a place to call home. Mr Kalin charges far too much rent, but that only makes Naveed more determined to work harder and longer. After all, he is the man of the house now, the head of the family. It is all up to him.

He grits his teeth. Improvements, that's what they need. He'll make improvements to the room as soon as possible. A proper door to keep out the icy winds when they return next year. A thick mat for the earthen floor. A good charcoal burner for cooking and heating. The kerosene cooker they have now is old and dangerous.

Yes, that's it, improvements. Little by little he will turn this room into a real home. *Qatra qatra darya mesha*, as Padar would say. *Drop by drop a river is made.*

Naveed stretches, lifting his backside off the hard floor. That's another thing he'll get when they can afford it – a toshak, a proper sleeping mat. All he has now is a piece of cardboard. He dreams of owning a really soft toshak like his little sister's. Her sleeping mat comes from his grandmother and has extra padding. But then Anoosheh needs that; it helps her sleep when the pain becomes too great.

He glances across at his sister. She is sound asleep, curled up like a little ball. She cried out in the night, but then she usually does. His mother is asleep too. They look so peaceful it sends a rush of warmth through him, making him smile. They are the biggest reason he has to be thankful. They are his reason for living.

A second explosion startles Naveed, quickly followed by a third. Both blasts make the ground tremble, though they still don't wake his mother and sister. At least he now knows that the first explosion was real, and where it had come from.

Definitely not Taliban; too big for them. The blasts were from Bagram Airfield, the huge American base about five kilometres away. The Americans liked blowing up things. They did it all the time.

He waits for more explosions. But they don't come. The aeroplanes continue, though; they will go on for a long time now. Bagram Airfield has been rumbling and grumbling every day of late, and well into the night. The Americans are leaving, flying out machinery, weapons and equipment every chance they get. It is said that by the end of the year the main forces will be gone, and Afghans will be in charge of their own future. Naveed can't imagine what that will be like; the Americans have been part of his life for as long as he can remember.

They came when he was only a year and a half old, after decades of struggle and strife – war with the Russians, civil war with the Mujaheddin, the cruel rule of the Taliban. Naveed's father had been thrilled at the time.

I knew there was a reason we called you Naveed, he used to say. The name meant 'good news, happy tidings'. *It was Allah's way of telling us not to give up hope.*

And at first the Americans were like a fresh breeze. They promised peace and stability. They promised to rebuild the country, a brand new Afghanistan where people could do and think and say whatever they wanted. Afghans began to hope once more.

That was thirteen years ago. How sour things had turned. The peace didn't last long, the stability crumbled to desert dust. The great wealth that poured into the country was swallowed by foreign companies and local warlords; ordinary Afghans saw none of it.

And now, after all those years and all that promise, the Americans are leaving.

Good news? Happy tidings? Sometimes Naveed feels his name is like a bad joke.

He stands, waiting for another sound, one that always comes at this time in the morning, as sure as the sun rises. He walks across the room to the doorway, lifts the blanket and steps through into a small outside alcove that separates the room from the passing alley.

On a rickety table is a basin, beside it a jug of water. He pours a little of the chill liquid into the basin and begins making wud'u, cleansing himself for prayer, for the sake of Allah.

When finished washing, he stands up straight and takes a deep breath, waiting, anticipating.

A moment later, there it is.

'Allahu Akbar.'

The voice of the muezzin wafts from the mosque on the other side of town, calling everyone to the first prayers of the day, the Namaaz e Sohb.

'Allahu Akbar.'

The azan, the call to prayer, rings out again, and twice more, followed by further declarations from the muezzin in a long melodic song drifting through the air, beckoning to all.

Naveed listens, entranced by the beauty of the muezzin's voice. When the azan is finished, he raises his hands in the air and, facing Mecca, whispers the words himself.

'Allahu Akbar.'

Then, his hands folded across his chest, he begins to pray. He has much to thank Allah for.

And maybe a few favours to ask.

Chapter 2

'Little sister, please.'

Naveed claps his hands at Anoosheh, amused at her playfulness but also aware of the time.

'Ajala kon – hurry up! We have to go.'

Ever since breakfast his sister has been cavorting around on her crutches, spinning and twisting. Naveed made some adjustments to them yesterday, adding soft underarm pads and new bases with rubber he'd found among the rubbish near the bazaar.

'They're perfect,' she laughs. 'Thank you, baradar-e bozorg, big brother.' She spins past him. He tries to catch her but she keeps just out of reach, performing a pirouette on her newly improved crutches.

Naveed rolls his eyes, exasperated but unable to be annoyed. Anoosheh is the joy of his life, a constant source of fun and laughter despite all that's happened. Five years have passed since she lost her legs. Amputated just above the knees. An improvised explosive device. Naveed won't ever forget, not any of it. He can still hear

7

the explosion, still see her crumple like a ragdoll. It is part of the darkness he carries, the darkness that fell upon him that day – a pall of horror and sadness for his little sister. And guilt, for she had been in his care. Why had he let her run ahead? Why couldn't he have been the one to step on the IED? Such questions have stabbed him like daggers ever since.

And yet over the years Anoosheh has never looked at him with even a hint of blame. Nor has she ever shown any sign of self-pity. Not once. The opposite, in fact.

'I'm warning you, Noosh.' He tries to sound threatening, but his sister only laughs. So he pretends to be a barmanu, one of the giant creatures said to live in the caves of the Hindu Kush, and begins chasing her. 'You asked for it. I eat young girls. Grrrrr!'

'Komak! Help! Keep away,' she squeals and scampers off. Naveed is amazed at how quickly she can move using a combination of her stumpy legs and crutches.

'Really, Anoosheh! I have to go,' he insists. 'I'll be late for work and you'll be late for school.'

'Huh! Work? School?' she shouts dismissively. 'We won't need either of those when I'm a famous hip-hop dancer.'

'Oh? So is that what you're going to be now?' her mother asks. 'I thought it was a ballerina.'

'That was ages ago, Madar. Hip hop is much better, and I think I have a natural talent for it. Have you seen my latest move? Watch.'

She tosses the crutches away and stands on her two stumpy legs, using her hands to balance. Before anyone can stop her, she drops to her back on the earthen floor and begins to spin. Her mother springs forward at once.

'Ayee!' she yells, grabbing her daughter and lifting her up. 'Don't you dare. That's your one clean outfit. It's for school, not for rolling in the dirt like a pig.'

'Madar!' Anoosheh cries, wriggling to free herself. 'How will I ever become Afghanistan's Queen of Hip Hop if you won't let me practise?'

'Enough, daughter. Your brother is right. Off to school with you. Go, now!'

Anoosheh stops struggling. She throws her arms around her mother's neck, hugging and kissing her. 'Khoda hafez, goodbye, Madar.'

Naveed picks up the crutches, tossing them to his sister one after the other. She turns in her mother's arms, catches them, and is about to rush off, but her mother pulls her back.

'Wait, you little worm,' she says, wrapping a thick scarf around Anoosheh's neck. 'There's a cold wind out there. You won't be hipping or hopping anywhere if you don't look after those lungs of yours.'

Anoosheh huffs impatiently as her mother also makes sure her headscarf is tied securely and her coat buttoned up. Then she scuttles out the door as fast as a cockroach. 'Come along, baradar,' she shouts. 'Keep up. You're as slow as a snail.'

Naveed shakes his head, then throws Anoosheh's satchel over his shoulder, along with his own bag, and kisses his mother.

9

'Khoda hafez, Madar. I will bring home food for tonight, and hopefully some money, if God wills it.'

'You are a good boy, Naveed. Anoosheh and I are fortunate to have you.'

'Not nearly as fortunate as we are to have you, Madar.'

Naveed's mother reaches out and strokes his cheek. A shadow of concern drifts across her face like a grey cloud. 'Whatever happens, I only hope that—' She cuts herself short and looks away.

'What is it, Madar?'

'Hich,' she whispers, keeping her face averted. 'Nothing.'

'Madar, please,' Naveed insists. 'Look at me.'

She eventually turns her face to him. She is smiling sweetly now, but Naveed guesses it is only with her lips. She has always made a point of hiding her sad feelings, never wishing to burden him or Anoosheh with her worries. He sees that her eyes glisten.

'What is the matter?' he persists. 'Tell me.'

She shakes her head. 'Man hoob hastam, I'm fine. Really, my son, I am.'

Naveed doesn't believe a word of it, but before he can question her further the blanket covering the doorway is swept aside and Anoosheh appears.

'Are you coming, baradar?' she snaps. Then, mimicking his voice perfectly, she adds: 'I'll be late for school and you'll be late for work.'

Their mother bursts out laughing. 'Take her away, my son. Please, I beg of you!'

10

Chapter 3

Because they're in a hurry, Anoosheh and Naveed take a shortcut to school. It snakes through lanes and alleys where some of the poorest of Bagram live – in crumbling mud huts, tents and derelict hovels. The long war has created a vast army of the desperate and starving – widows with children they can't possibly feed; legions of street kids, abandoned or orphaned.

They pass vacant lots piled high with stinking garbage, through narrow unpaved streets with potholes and open sewage drains. Impossibly thin wild-eyed children, sit in the rubbish as if they are part of it. A few squat by the drains, staring at Naveed and his sister as they pass, too lethargic to move. One boy calls to them.

'Az barai khuda, ghareeb hastam – for God's sake, I am poor.'

Naveed and Anoosheh want to help. They can see that the boy is starving. But they have nothing themselves. And they know that if they do help, they'll be swamped by the other children. They keep moving.

Eventually they reach a much wider street, one which is paved, although the surface is broken in places, cracks all through it. This street joins the main road that comes from the city of Charikar in the north-west and leads to the centre of Bagram. In the other direction is one of the richest parts of town, where warlords and drug barons and anyone else able to skim off some of the foreign wealth pouring into Afghanistan live in brash palace-like mansions.

'Nearly there,' says Naveed as they turn into the street. The school is only a hundred metres away. Anoosheh hurries ahead of her brother. 'Be careful,' he shouts.

Naveed is not overly worried. Anoosheh is remarkably capable on her crutches, and generally aware of her surroundings. Besides, she is barely ten metres ahead of him, and the traffic is only light at present. Even so, he instinctively quickens his pace, and calls again.

'Anoosheh. Slow down.'

As the words leave his lips, there is a roar from behind. Naveed whips his head around to see a huge black Humvee bearing down at full speed – a warlord's warhorse. He sprints after Anoosheh, shouting. She stops and turns, but one of her crutches slips into a crack and lodges there. She topples sideways, sprawling onto the road, right in the path of the Humvee.

'Anoosheh!'

Naveed hurls himself at his sister, grabbing her outstretched hand and dragging her off the road as the Humvee snarls past. A second later and the black beast would have driven straight over Anoosheh.

Naveed lies on his back at the side of the road, eyes shut, taking deep breaths. His sister lies on top of him. He still has her hand clenched firmly in his.

'Ayee, little Noosh!' he mutters weakly.

He opens his eyes and stares straight into hers. They are full of gratitude.

'God is kind to bless me with a brother like you.' She hugs him hard.

A crowd has formed. People peer down at them, concerned. Naveed lifts his sister off and stands, helping her up. Then he retrieves Anoosheh's crutches and hands them to her.

'A thousand curses,' she shouts after the Humvee, even though it has long since vanished down the road. Everyone knows that the big black vehicle belongs to one or other of the warlords or drug barons in the area, and they all nod in agreement.

'May your eyes fall out and your teeth go black!' Anoosheh continues. 'May your skin be covered in scabs!' She shakes her fist in the air. 'Coward!' she yells, almost toppling sideways in the process.

The crowd cheers and Naveed smiles. He does wonder where Anoosheh learned such a curse, but loves the fierce pride that burns in her, making her seem tall.

'Come along, sister,' he says. 'I've had enough excitement for one morning.'

Anoosheh's friend Pari is waiting as they pass through the gate into the school.

'I thought you'd never come,' she says. 'What kept you?'

'Brothers,' Anoosheh says, clicking her tongue. 'I swear he slept in.'

'Noosh!' Naveed gapes at his sister.

Pari laughs. She knows what Anoosheh is like. They've been friends for a long time, even though Pari is about two years older, nearly thirteen.

'And then I couldn't get him out of the house,' Anoosheh goes on, grinning wickedly.

'Stop it, sister.' Naveed becomes flustered. 'Tell her the truth.'

'But the truth is so boring. It always ruins a good story.'

Pari laughs, tossing her head back. Naveed notices her slender neck and tries to look away. But then she smiles at him, and now there is nowhere else Naveed can look. Her teeth are so white, and perfect like her lips. Her deep green eyes are the shape of almonds.

'Actually the truth isn't boring at all this time,' Anoosheh continues. 'I was nearly killed.'

Pari stares wide-eyed at her young friend. 'Nearly killed?' she asks. 'How? Where?'

'I'll tell you later,' Anoosheh replies. 'But it's the truth. I'd be dead but for Naveed.' Her voice softens slightly. 'He saved my life.' She gives him a thump. 'There. Satisfied, big brother?'

Suddenly Naveed feels very self-conscious. He gazes at the two girls until his sister gives him another thump.

'Well, don't just stand there like a love-struck monkey. You'll be late for work if you don't hurry.' Anoosheh then tugs at Pari. 'And we'll be late for lessons. Come. See you this afternoon, brother.'

Naveed watches the girls go, then turns to leave.

'She is quite a character, your sister.'

The school principal is standing in his path.

'Mr Farzin, sir. Salaam alaikum.'

'And peace be upon you, Naveed. You are not staying? We would love to have you here.'

Naveed flinches. He hasn't attended school for four years now, ever since his father was killed. The memory is still raw, and easily triggered.

He was calling to his father from the other side of the market when it happened.

Padar!

He can still hear his own scream as if it is locked in his head. He can still see his father blown to pieces. Again the horror, as with Anoosheh. Again the pain. Again the guilt, for he'd been troublesome that day, running off and hiding among the stalls, not coming when called, yelling from the other side of the market, teasing his father.

Padar!

More darkness seeping into his mind, slowly eating away at him.

'I would love to come back, sir,' Naveed replies, pushing the darkness aside. 'But I must work. We need to eat.'

'I understand, my boy. It is a great pity, though. You were my best student.' Mr Farzin rests his hand on Naveed's shoulder. 'Just remember: our door is always open to you.'

'Thank you, Mr Farzin. I will not forget. Perhaps one day, Allah willing.'

'I hope so. We need someone to keep Anoosheh under control.' They both laugh. The principal then pats Naveed reassuringly on the back. 'Off you go.'

Naveed walks away. At the gate he pauses. The traffic is much busier now. He takes a deep breath. He has to make his way to the bustling community that has grown up around Bagram Airfield several kilometres away. As if reminding him of this, a jet plane that has just taken off from the base screams overhead. He blocks his ears, knowing that two or three more will be close behind.

Chapter 4

A Strike Eagle fighter jet howls down the runway and hurtles into the sky, quickly followed by another. And another. In next to no time the sleek war birds are mere dots on the horizon. Deadly dots. Seconds later a C-17 Globemaster III lands with a giant's roar. No sooner has it touched down, its huge bulk lumbering along the airstrip, than two HH-60 choppers armed with twin cannons and carrying a medivac team *thud-thud* away on a rescue mission, and a wise old CH-47 Chinook adds its voice to the great concert of war.

Jake Ryan stands outside his B-hut, transfixed by the sound and fury. Even after more than six months at Bagram Airfield, the young Australian explosives expert is still amazed by the awesome display of power.

An American soldier from the same B-hut, Private Horten, punches at the sky as he passes. 'Impressive, huh?' he shouts. 'That's the US of A, bud, telling all them Talibs to back off or we'll bake 'em good!'

It is impressive, Jake has to agree: a mega-show of

military might. But are the Taliban backing off? He wonders. It actually looks to him as if the boot could be on the other foot.

Over at one of the tarmacs a long line of turtleback Humvees are being loaded onto a huge transport carrier. This time last year those squat armour-plated hogs would have been heading off to battle. A regiment of soldiers marches by, acknowledging a superior officer with their characteristic 'Hoo Har' as they head for a troop carrier that will fly them home. It's happening all the time now; more and more troops and equipment are being shipped out. The end game is on.

'Ready to go, Stingray?' Jake leans down and pats the black and tan kelpie at his side. The dog seems to smile. 'Come on, mate. Time for our run.'

Jake swings his M16 over his shoulder and sets off along Disney Drive, the main thoroughfare through the base from north to south.

He pushes himself hard, only stopping when he reaches the main perimeter road near the edge of the base. Glancing up, his gaze settles on the Hindu Kush. The mountains glare down on the base like ancient warriors, their snow-covered peaks glowing in the morning sun with timeless, silent dignity.

A light breeze blows across the Shomali Plain. It will later stiffen, bringing dust. But for now it merely rattles the small metal tags printed with skull and crossbones that hang from the fence. Jake knows their sound well. He shifts his gaze from the mountains to the fence and through it to the fields beyond.

In the distance he can see the scrappy villages. Closer, a herd of goats graze on the early spring grasses. Closer still, a woman passes by, her blue burqa piled high with twigs, while a rabble of boys play soccer with a plastic bottle. Scattered across this scene like scabs are the wrecks of Russians tanks, MiGs and APCs, rusting reminders of another war fought on Afghan soil. And peppered among it all are the hidden killers left behind by that war – landmines. Jake's immediate instinct is to call out, but something else catches his eye.

A lone figure stands in the field about midway between the fence and the boys playing soccer – a man, his clothes the colour of the earth, his skin a shade darker. Tall, he stands erect like a guard on duty, with sharp angular features that might have been carved from the Hindu Kush. An old mujaheddin, Jake decides.

The man turns his head, a rapid movement that catches Jake out. Embarrassed, he smiles weakly and nods. But the old warrior stares right through him. Then, with a slight toss of his head, he turns away, picks up his hoe and continues digging.

Jake watches for a moment longer, then walks off. He doesn't feel like running anymore.

The breeze lifts, the skull-and-crossbone tags dance, and the air base rages louder than ever.

But the old warrior keeps chipping away.

Chapter 5

After leaving the school Naveed makes his way across the street. Cars and trucks blow their horns and men shout, but no one slows down. He has to zigzag through the traffic, knowing when to stand statue-still and when to sprint like a hare. Twice he is almost run over, but eventually makes it to the other side and continues up the street until he reaches the big road from Charikar.

That road is busier still as it heads into Bagram. Cars crammed with passengers jostle utilities, jingle trucks, motorbikes and military vehicles in a screeching, squawking battle to stay on the road. Donkeys with huge loads on their backs, or pulling carts filled to the limit, trot silently along at the edge of the road, heads bowed in ancient submission. And scattered among it all are the people.

Naveed weaves his way through a crowd of vendors pulling carts and pushing trolleys, past boys lugging bundles as big as themselves. He skirts around women in burqas tugging children and clutching babies. He passes merchants dressed in their best loonges and perahan toombon – turbans with trousers and matching long shirts – and farmers with sheep hung around their necks.

'Navi!' He hears his name above the hubbub and looks about. 'Over here.'

The voice comes from a jingle truck some way back in the traffic. Naveed turns to see the brightly coloured vehicle, painted all over with gaudy images, covered in baubles and bells and jangling chains. A young man hangs out the window waving with his free arm.

'Hurry up, I'll give you a lift.'

Naveed's face brightens and he pushes through the people to the edge of the road. The truck slows down as it draws level with him, but only enough for him to run alongside and scramble up onto the running board.

'Fariad,' he shouts, grinning broadly. 'Hello, my friend.'

The young man grasps Naveed's arm in greeting. 'Long time no see. How are you?'

'Good. And you?'

'Well, I'm a truck driver now, aren't I?' Fariad puffs out his chest. 'That means hard work, long hours, bad coffee and getting *plenty* angry.' As if to prove his point, Fariad slams his hand on the horn and shouts out the window at a motorbike that has swerved in front of him. 'Antar, mashang, korreh khar! – baboon, retard, son of a donkey!' But in the next breath he adds: 'It's great. Always something happening, never boring. And the money's good.' He rubs his thumb and

21

fingers together, but then in the same move shoves his middle finger in the air at a passing car. 'Gom sho – get lost!'

Naveed cannot help laughing. He's not seen Fariad for over six months, and he can feel his spirits lifting in response to all the energy and zest for life bubbling from him. The young man is not a *man* at all, really – seventeen years old at the most – but tall and very mature for his age. Naveed can already detect the shadowy beginnings of a beard.

'It's so good to see you,' he says. 'Are you here for long?'

Fariad shakes his head. 'Just passing through. A load for Bagram Airfield then straight on to Kabul for a Kandahar job – all for the American devils. I'll be sad when they go; they're good for business.' He hangs out the window again. 'Uhmnq – idiot!' Then he grins at Naveed. 'But I'll be back.'

'Good. Then you should join us for a meal.'

'I'd like that.'

'We have a house now,' Naveed adds. 'Well, just a room really.'

'Wonderful. How is your mother?'

'Better. But Padar is in her thoughts every day. It's the same for me. The emptiness is—'

'I know what you mean,' Fariad interrupts.

Naveed bites his lip. 'Of course you do. Bebakhshid. Forgive me.'

Fariad waves his hand dismissively, but Naveed still feels terrible.

He and Fariad had been friends as children. They used to play in the same street. Those were happy days, before tragedy struck. Fariad's family – mother, father and two sisters – were killed by a suicide bomber. On a bus. A day trip to Charikar for a kite-flying competition; Fariad was a champion sky lord with a brand new kite. When the bus stopped for fuel on the outskirts of Bagram, Fariad's father sent him to buy sweets for the family from a vendor. As the boy got off the bus, the bomber got on. They passed. They probably touched. Their eyes might even have met.

The blast killed everyone on the bus. It killed the vendor as well. Fariad survived because he was shielded by the tall trolley of sweets. He spent many months in the American hospital at Bagram Airfield, his body covered in wounds and burns. The long scar Naveed now notices down the side of his face is but one of them. The beard will help to hide that when it grows.

'And what about little Noosh?' Fariad asks. 'Still a terrorist?'

'Worse than ever. She wages jihad on me every day, I swear.'

Fariad laughs and then glances wistfully at Naveed. 'You're right. It is a pity I can't stay. I'd love to. Maybe one day.'

Naveed knows that Fariad keeps his sadness buried deep inside, so deep that most people wouldn't even have a clue it was there. But in that glance he catches a tiny glimpse of his friend's real pain. He tries to change the subject.

'What an exciting life you lead now,' he blurts. 'I envy you.'

'Well, don't. I like my job, yes. It's exciting and fun, and the hard work stops me thinking too much. But let me tell you this: I would toss it all away in a flash if I could get back even *some* of what once was mine. There are sparkles and bright lights in my life, yes, but yours is filled with *real* treasure.'

There is nothing Naveed can say to this. He simply rests his hand on Fariad's arm and they travel down the road in silence for a while, each lost in thought. All too soon they near the centre of Bagram.

'I have to go,' Naveed says, his words steeped in regret.

He prepares to jump off as they near the market area, but doesn't want to. Meeting Fariad has made him feel so good. It has chased away the grey clouds that seemed to be gathering at the edge of his life. If only the bright moments could be captured and kept in a bottle, he wishes, to be sipped at in darker times. If only . . .

'Don't fret, Navi,' Fariad says, as though reading his friend's thoughts. 'We'll meet again. I'm sure of it.' He presses his fist against the boy's chin and then gives him a playful shove.

Naveed leaps off and runs alongside the truck for a bit before slowing to a stop. The gaudy vehicle jingle-jangles away in a cloud of diesel smoke, Fariad's smiling face framed in the side mirror. Naveed waves. Fariad pokes his arm out the window and waves back. But in the next instant he's shaking his fist and cursing someone.

24

'Your face looks like a monkey's bum!' he yells, and rattles on down the road to Bagram Airfield.

Naveed can see the vast military complex now, little more than a kilometre away, its control tower poking up like a concrete fist. An enormous troop-carrier aircraft is just coming in to land, its roar drowning out the traffic noise.

Naveed watches the big metal bird for a moment, then turns and plunges into the crowd.

Chapter 6

'Sorry I'm late, Mr Waleed.'

'Mohem nist, Naveed, no problem. Time is of little importance in the grand scheme.'

Mr Waleed is a small, plump man with a face made for smiles and a disposition to match. His shop in the central area of Bagram sells a bit of everything – a sort of general store, only more. It is said that if Mr Waleed can't get something for you, nobody can.

The store is the first place Naveed visits each morning on his search for work. The friendly shopkeeper always has at least a few chores for him and always pays: mostly in cash, sometimes in kind.

'Any jobs today, Mr Waleed?' he asks.

'Certainly, my boy; quite a few, in fact. Shelves to stack, aisles to sweep. The front pavement could do with a good scrub, and the windows are overdue for a clean. But I'll get you to do the deliveries first.'

Naveed knows the routine well; he's worked for Mr Waleed for about a year and a half. He goes straight to a trolley full of parcels waiting near the front of the store. There are more than usual today.

'Here, eat these on the way,' says Mr Waleed, handing Naveed a couple of large mantu. 'You'll need the energy with that load.'

Naveed gladly accepts the warm meat dumplings and begins eating as he pushes the trolley out the door. But even though he is hungry – he only had a piece of stale nan bread for breakfast – he doesn't gobble down the mantu. He eats the first one slowly, savouring each bite of the spicy ground beef and the tasty seer moss, the white garlic sauce drizzled on top. And he only eats a little of the second dumpling, keeping the rest for later. Then he heads off on his deliveries, pleased that the empty feeling has been chased from his stomach.

He moves quickly on his rounds, pushing the trolley at a jog. Most of the deliveries are within a kilometre of the town centre. As he drops off each parcel he waits briefly for a tip, a small coin usually. There's no obligation to give him anything, and quite a few don't. He will sometimes wait longer if he feels he deserves payment, such as when he's delivered a particularly heavy parcel. But even then he can leave empty-handed.

This morning has been reasonable, though, Naveed decides, after dropping off the last parcel and collecting another coin for his effort. He counts his money: twelve afghanis so far, a good start to the day. He takes a small pouch from around his neck and slips the coins into it. The pouch was his father's. He runs his fingers fondly over its soft leather before placing it around his neck again and securing his top button. Then he leans against the trolley and takes out the rest of the mantu. But just as he raises it to his mouth he sees the dog.

It's her, the dog that's been following him for a couple of months now, ever since he gave her a bone he found in the garbage at the back of a restaurant. He's fed her a few times since, only scraps, but enough to make her lock onto him. She's not been around for the last few days, and he had assumed she'd left. But here she is again, standing about twenty metres away in the shadow of a truck, her whitish coat giving her a ghostlike quality.

She's a tall dog, about eighty centimetres at the withers, with a big head, straight back and thick neck. The hair on her body is of medium length, a strip of longer hair down the middle of her back. She looks as if she could have strayed from some Kuchis, passing nomads, and become lost. A mastiff bred for the steppes or mountains, she is not coping at all well in the city. She should be quite a heavy dog, but her body is bony, thinner than last time they met, her ribs showing, and Naveed can see the hunger in her eyes as she stares at him.

That stare makes him pause with the dumpling almost in his mouth. A few quick chomps and it would be gone, he thinks but then lowers his hand instead.

'Very well,' he mutters and walks towards the dog. 'You need it more than me.'

When he's about five metres away, she sits, as she has every time he's fed her. She seems to have been well trained at some stage, used to obeying and keen to please. And now it's almost as if she's decided to take him on as her new master. Even when he places the mantu on the ground she doesn't rush forward, despite her obvious hunger. She waits until he retreats to the trolley and nods. Then she goes straight to the dumpling and quickly devours it, licking at the ground for a while to get every last morsel. A moment later she turns her big sad eyes on Naveed again, asking for more.

'Sorry, it's all I have,' he says. 'And it won't do you any good looking at me like that. I have enough trouble feeding myself and my family.'

The dog keeps her gaze on him. Naveed stares into her eyes, feeling oddly captivated by them. Then he shakes his head, suddenly annoyed with himself. Why is he wasting time talking to a dog? He has to make more than twelve afghanis if they're going to eat tonight. He turns and walks away.

The dog watches him go, sniffs the spot where the dumpling had been, and leaves as well.

When Naveed returns to Mr Waleed's, he quickly sets about doing the other jobs the shopkeeper has for him. He stacks the shelves and sweeps the aisles. He scrubs and washes the pavement outside the shop, then cleans and polishes the front window until it is spotless. When he steps back to inspect his work, he notices his own reflection in the glass, and is immediately shocked by how poor he looks.

His clothes come from a charity pool, discarded garments from overseas. His mother got them almost a year ago but is having trouble finding more now that the charity has closed. The dirty canvas sandshoes are old and tatty, his toes poking out of one of them. The brown trackpants are patched on both knees and too short for his growing legs. He likes the warmth of his maroon woollen jumper, but it is definitely too small. He even needs a new beanie; it barely covers his ears.

As Naveed gazes into the window, he imagines how wonderful it would be to have some good clothes, proper Afghan ones. He can just see himself in his own perahan toombon with a chapan coat like President Karzai's, topped off with a karakul hat and scarf also like the ones worn by the president. He turns sideways, imagining himself in such finery.

'What's this, then?' Mr Waleed's portly figure appears in the window. 'Admiring yourself?'

Naveed laughs nervously. 'I'm just giving it a final check.' He pretends to spy a smudge, and springs forward, buffing the window briskly with his cloth. 'There.' He stands back. 'All done. Anything else, Mr Waleed?'

'Not today, but there should be more deliveries tomorrow. Mind you, business is not quite as brisk as it used to be, now that the foreigners are running away.' Mr Waleed presses a few coins into Naveed's hand – another twenty afghanis. Then he gives him a brown paper package. 'A few more of those mantu,' he explains. 'Mrs Waleed always cooks far too many for me.'

Naveed dips his head. 'You are too kind, sir.'

Chapter 7

Naveed has many more places he can visit for work. It's a matter of where he will make the best money for the time he has left in the day.

He decides to check out Mr Hadi's chai house next, and arrives with seconds to spare before the lunchtime deliveries begin. Mr Hadi is known for his excellent teas – shir chai and others – as well as a wide assortment of sweets and pastries. Offices and shops in the area order from him throughout the day, so there's often work for chai boys.

A crowd of boys are already milling around the chai house when Naveed arrives. But he has a good name among the customers; his service is prompt and efficient, he never spills anything, and he's always respectful. Mr Hadi knows this and beckons him at once, sending him off with one of the first trays.

Naveed works quickly, managing to deliver three more trays before the lunchtime rush is over. When finished, he looks for Mr Hadi and finds him in the kitchen. The café owner sits at a table, hunched over a small radio. He has the volume low and is listening so intently that he doesn't even notice Naveed.

'Hear me, fellow Afghans.'

Naveed immediately recognises the woman's voice on the radio. It is the politician for peace, the great Malalai Farzana. For over a year now she has been talking to ordinary Afghans, many of whom long for peace. She broadcasts speeches on radio and television, and travels to remote areas at great personal risk, talking to anyone who will listen. Loved by the ordinary people, hated by extremists and the powerful, she is called the Voice of the Voiceless.

'The foreign forces are leaving Afghanistan,' Malalai Farzana continues. 'Each day more of them go. By the end of the year, there will be few left. It is what we want – to take charge of our own destiny. But it will not be easy. More than ever we must think as one people, not as Pashtuns, Tajiks, Hindus, Uzbeks, Hazaras and so on. That is how the enemies of peace want us to think – the warlords and drug barons and the Taliban – so they can divide and rule us. Believe me, while ever we remain separate tribes the winter of war will chill our land and our very souls. We are all Afghans. Never forget that idea. Hold it in your hearts, for within it lies our future.'

Mr Hadi flicks off the radio and glances up at Naveed. 'That is a wonderful woman, my boy, a real force for good and hope. She speaks wisely. May Allah watch over her.' He sips at his chai for a moment, frowning. 'But I do fear what might happen when the foreigners leave. I fear that the enemies of peace will have their way.'

Naveed leaves the chai house with Malalai Farzana's words at the back of his mind and fifteen more afghanis in his father's leather pouch. He decides on a car wash as his last stop for the day. There's a new one on the way home, and he reckons he can do three or four cars before he has to pick up Anoosheh from school.

To his delight, he washes five cars in the time available. But the manager finds fault with two of them and only pays for three. It's an old trick, and Naveed would normally protest. But he's tired and doesn't have time to argue; he's already late for his sister. He makes a mental note to put the car wash on his black list, and accepts the money with a polite smile.

Then he runs. The school is about a kilometre away, and he should be there by now. He knows that Anoosheh will be fine. Pari will wait with her if need be. And then there's Mr Farzin; the principal would never leave Anoosheh on her own. But that's not the point. She is his sister, his responsibility. He has a duty to be there for her.

❖❖❖

'This is heaven,' Naveed murmurs.

He lies on Anoosheh's toshak, eyes closed. His head rests in her lap as she gently massages his neck while his mother massages his tired, sore feet. She has already washed them with hot water, smoothing a little ointment

34

into the blisters, and now draws out the aches and pains with exquisite skill.

Your mother has hands of magic. Naveed recalls his father's words as he lies back.

'Of course it's heaven, brother,' says Anoosheh. 'You're in the very best of hands. Mind you, we're not cheap. We charge by the minute, you know.'

Naveed chuckles. It is wonderful having the two people he loves the most fuss over him so tenderly. A perfect end to a good day. Meeting Fariad was such a delight that Naveed still feels boosted by it. And then the work was good; he made decent money and bought food with Anoosheh on the way home. They will eat well tonight, and for the next day or two provided they're careful. The rest of his earnings went towards the rent; they now have the next month's payment in hand. That alone is a great relief.

'Allah is kind to me.'

Naveed opens his eyes a little, enough to see his mother. She works vigorously at his feet, pressing hard with her fingers, pushing with her thumbs. Her hair is swept back, revealing her high, wide brow and strong features. *Your mother is the most beautiful woman in the world*, his father used to say, and Naveed can see what he meant. But he can also see the lines of worry on her brow, the same ones which were there that morning.

'What's the problem, Madar?'

'Hich,' she mutters and shakes her head dismissively.

'You said that this morning, but it isn't nothing, I can tell. You also said: *Whatever happens, I only hope*

35

that ... But you didn't finish. What did you mean, Madar? I won't give up until you tell me.'

Naveed's mother stops massaging and flicks her large black eyes up at him.

'The future – what lies ahead for us, for you and Anoosheh in particular – that's what worries me now the foreigners are leaving. I can only see darkness.'

'No, Madar, it doesn't have to be that way. I heard Malalai Farzana again today, on the radio at Mr Hadi's. She says it will be good, the foreigners leaving. It will mean we can decide our own future for a change. She says we have to pull together as one people, not as a lot of tribes.'

'That's the problem, my son: we *are a lot of tribes*. And because of that, the Taliban will certainly return, strangling any joy we might ever have hoped for in life. They're waiting to pounce. They'll squabble with the warlords over this carcass of a country, as they've always done. It's just an endless game of buzkashi.'

Naveed hears the sadness in his mother's voice, and sees the anguish glisten in her eyes. He gets to his knees and hugs her. 'Don't fret. I will look after you, always.'

'Oh yes, I know you will, as best you can. But these are big forces, Naveed. We're nothing to them, nobodies. When elephants fight, the grass gets trampled.'

'Madar!' Anoosheh exclaims, rushing to her mother's side as well. 'What would Padar think of such talk? You told me he said we must always seek the light. Look for the jewels in life and you'll be rich. If you only ever stare into the dark corners you'll never see anything.'

'Of course.' Her mother takes a deep breath, pulling herself together. 'How silly of me.'

'Exactly.' Anoosheh claps her hands together. 'Besides, I think our hard-working man of the house needs feeding.'

'You're right, little one. And what good things you two bought. We'll eat like khans tonight, thanks to you, my son. Your father would be proud of you.'

She kisses Naveed on the forehead and rises from the toshak, holding up her hand when he moves to stand as well.

'No. Stay where you are. You need your rest.'

Naveed is only too happy to do what his mother bids. As she and Anoosheh set to chopping the vegetables and spicing the meat, he eases back on the delectably soft toshak, lets his head sink into the pillows, and closes his eyes.

Chapter 8

'Good onya, mate. You're the best.'

Jake pats Stingray and rubs his muzzle. Then he slowly slides his hand into his pocket. The dog stares up expectantly, tail wagging.

'Guess what I've got?'

Ears pricked, the kelpie trembles as Jake slowly pulls out the very thing he's been waiting for . . . a ball. *His* ball! Stingray barks and drops onto his front paws as Jake leans back and hurls the little round thing into the air. The dog is after it in a flash.

This is his reward. It's even more of a reward than any special bits of food he might receive when he's performed well. For him the ball is sheer excitement. He will run after it and fetch it back for as long as Jake keeps throwing. And this is what makes him a good explosive detection dog, his unquenchable love of chasing and retrieving. It's one of the most important qualities in such a dog, and Stingray has it in buckets.

Jake continues tossing the ball as he walks towards the southern entry control point for Bagram Airfield, smiling all the way. He's so pleased with the kelpie. They've just finished a week of specialised training in explosives detection, and Stingray has shone at every stage.

'You were amazing, mate,' Jake says as he takes the saliva-covered ball from Stingray's jaws and throws it yet again, shouting out loud, 'AMAZING!'

'Someone's happy.'

Jake has reached the entry control point with its maze of Hesco barriers and concrete blast panels, manned machine-gun posts and armoured Humvees at the ready. Four American soldiers and a few Afghan trainees stand about. The voice comes from Private Horten, the American soldier from Jake's B-hut.

'G'day, Horto,' Jake replies. 'You bet I'm happy. I've got the best sniffing mutt on the base.' Jake takes the ball from Stingray and pockets it this time. Then he clips on his lead. 'I'm taking him out for a taste of the real world.'

'Okay, but be careful. Those hajis might look harmless but there are some bad dudes among them.'

Jake raises an eyebrow. 'I'll be right, mate. The "hajis" have enough going on without worrying about me.'

'All right,' Horten says, raising his hands. 'Just be careful, that's all. I don't want no dead Aussie on my hands.' He thumps Jake on the arm. 'Now go on, git.'

Jake slips under the boom gate, past the busy bazaar the local merchants have set up outside the airfield, and heads straight down the avenue that leads off the base. Before long he is on a quiet tree-lined road, with orchards and tended fields on either side.

He unclips Stingray's leash and lets him go. The dog immediately comes to life. He darts from one new smell to another, loving his freedom, cocking his leg and leaving his mark at every stop. He pauses briefly to drink from a drain, and then is off again. Jake keeps a close eye on the dog, making sure he doesn't wander too far, but also wanting him to feel the sense of freedom that every dog should know.

They wander on until they come to a simple fence: a line of crooked steel posts about ten metres apart holding up one strand of sagging barbed wire. Jake tenses, seeing the red triangular landmine tags hanging from the wire at intervals. He stops, and gazes across a field riddled with Russian wrecks: tanks and trucks, cannons and ATVs. A huge transport carrier lies on its side like a beached whale, one wing poking up like a fin. About fifty metres away is the skeleton of a tank that has been picked to its bare bones.

Jake sighs, and is about to turn his back and carry on when he notices movement near the tank. He peers closer. It's a boy. On his knees. Digging.

'What the . . .' Jake mutters and then shouts, 'Hey. You.'

Chapter 9

Naveed hears the voice. He stops digging, straightens himself and looks over his shoulder. He sees the soldier waving his arms in the air and calling. He waves back but then goes on digging. He has one more piece to collect and then he'll be finished. He's been working here all morning, collecting Russian medals and military tags. The area is littered with them; it's like a gold mine. He pulls the last one from the soil and drops it into a hessian bag. Then he stands, stretches and waves to the soldier again.

'I come,' he shouts in English.

Naveed takes his time, eyes down, placing each step in a particular spot marked by a small stone. Only when he reaches the wobbly barbed-wire fence does he look up.

'Hello, sir. What you want?' he says with a broad smile. 'I help you?'

'Are you bloody mad?' Jake replies, trying to keep his voice down so he doesn't frighten the boy. 'Landmines. You know? Kaboom!' He throws his arms in the air.

41

'Yes, sir, I know kaboom. But I careful.' He points to the flattened grass and the stone markers for each footstep. 'I make good check of ground first.'

'I don't care how good you check. Those things can be really hidden. And they can kill you. At the very least they'll blow your legs off. Get me? No legs, no walk!'

Naveed grits his teeth. 'I know no legs, too.' His smile dims. 'Sir.'

'Stop calling me sir.'

'What I say then?'

'Just get out of that minefield first, eh? You're making me nervous.'

Naveed ducks under the barbed wire. 'So? What your name?'

'I'm Jake.'

'Hello, Mr Jake.' Naveed grasps Jake's hand and shakes it. 'I, Naveed.' He glances down at the kelpie. 'This your dog?'

'Yeah. He's Stingray.'

Naveed wrinkles his brow. 'Sting, er—?'

'Ray. It's a kind of fish.'

'But he dog.'

'Yeah, I know.' Jake shakes his head. 'It's a long story, mate.' He points at the hessian bag. 'What have you got in there?'

Naveed grins proudly and opens the bag wide, revealing the collection of medals and tags.

'You risked your life for a few scraps of rusty old metal?'

'I clean clean clean. Now no rust.' Naveed rubs his thumb and fingers together. 'You Americans pay good.'

'I'm Australian, mate, and it doesn't matter how good anyone pays. Nothing's worth the damage those things can do.' Jake points to the field. 'The Russians put them there, heaps of the buggers. Do you understand what I'm talking about? The Russians?'

Naveed understands exactly what Jake is talking about even though the Russians had come and gone well before he was even born. He knows because his father had been a resistance fighter as a young man and had battled the Russians to the bitter end. He used to talk with great sadness about the decade of war this plunged Afghanistan into. And he talked with even greater sorrow about the years of civil war that followed – of the warlords and the Taliban, Afghan killing Afghan – until the Americans came with their promise of hope.

And what had that promise come to? Some Afghans felt nothing much had really changed for ordinary people. Some even said things were worse now – more fighting, more killing, more orphans, more poverty, hunger, disease, more desperation.

'I understand.' Naveed stares straight at Jake. 'But always you have food,' he says slowly. 'Always you have house. But not Afghan people,' he adds, pausing to let his words sink in. 'Do *you* understand, Mr Jake?'

Jake is struck by the fierce intensity of the boy's eyes, the pride and defiance burning in them. They are the eyes of a much older person. And it's only then that Jake sees the threadbare clothes, the worn-out shoes, the thin face turned towards him. He suddenly feels embarrassed.

'I'm sorry,' he mutters. 'I didn't mean . . . There just has to be a better way, that's all.'

He rummages in his pockets, wishing he had some money to give the boy. All he can find are two energy bars. But Naveed shakes his head.

'No, no. I not take,' he says.

'Just take them, please.' Jake presses the bars into Naveed's hands. 'And tell me you won't go near those landmines again.'

Naveed smiles. 'Tashakor, Mr Jake. Thank you very much.' He picks up the bag and slings it over his shoulder. 'I go now. But I keep look out for you. And I keep look out for dog.' He pats the kelpie. 'Stingfish, yes?'

Jake chuckles. 'Yeah, that'll do.'

'Salaam alaikum, Mr Jake.'

'And peace be upon you, Naveed.'

Salaam alaikum. The words ring in Jake's mind as he watches the boy walk away. Such a futile expression in this war-ravaged land, where kids like him have only ever known fighting and killing, guns and bombs. *Peace be upon you.* If only it were that simple.

Chapter 10

That will do for now.

Naveed steps back from the wooden bench in the little alcove outside the room he calls home, and massages his aching fingers. Laid out before him are the Russian medals and badges he dug up near the American base earlier that day. He's worked tirelessly on them – washing, scrubbing, rubbing and brushing – gradually cleaning away the rust. Then endless polishing. He has kept at it all afternoon and well into the night, working by the light of the full moon to save kerosene; what little they have left is needed for cooking.

It is late. His mother and sister have been asleep for hours. Naveed is tired but still not ready to sleep himself. He's worried. He inspects his work, trying to keep his mind off his concerns. The medals look good. Some further polishing in the daylight, plus a coat of varnish given to him by Mr Waleed, and they will be ready. He will offer them for sale at the special market bazaar in town the day after tomorrow. American soldiers often come to that. God willing, they will buy the medals. He also has some Russian artillery and bullet shells that he hopes they will like.

This is only Naveed's second venture into the marketplace, but he knows he has to make as much money as possible on the day. He must arrive early, leave late, and sell hard all day. Last time he just managed to break even. He's determined to make a real profit this time. But he has to pay rent. The cheapest selling place in the bazaar is a hundred afghanis, a lot of money to him, for which he only gets an area slightly bigger than a metre square, plus a sheet of black plastic on which to display his goods.

As Naveed looks over his wares, he decides that he needs more items to sell if he's going to come away from the market with more than just a handful of afghanis. But there's only one day left to find those extra things. The best place to do that is the big waste disposal depot on the other side of the American air base. Naveed sighs, knowing that tomorrow won't be easy if that's where he's going.

His stomach groans. It's been groaning ever since the evening meal. All they had were potatoes, one each, and Naveed had given some of his to Anoosheh. She said no, but he insisted. There were also the energy bars, of course; he'd almost forgotten about those. They were delicious, but small, and they've worn off now, no more than a sweet memory.

Naveed closes his eyes. *Allah will look after us*, he tells himself.

What started out as a good week has turned into a bad one. He's had very little paid work – a few jobs for Mr Waleed and some car washing. That's all. A fire closed down Mr Hadi's chai house, and it will remain closed for many more days. It is said that his shop was targeted because he was a known sympathiser with the Americans.

There is the rent money, of course; that has been put aside. Naveed is tempted to dip into it for a little food, especially when he sees how hungry his sister and mother are. But he knows better.

Oh Padar, I'm no good at filling your shoes. Naveed steps from the alcove into the laneway. *When I see Madar and little Noosh hungry I ache inside. It's so hard just feeding ourselves, let alone finding the rent. And Mr Kalin gives no credit; he'd throw us out if we couldn't pay, I know he would.*

Naveed gazes up at the starry night, and sighs.

He's pestering Madar, too, you know? She will hardly talk about it, but the other day she told me he wants to take her as his wife. How dare he? She would be wife number three, a nobody, a slave. She doesn't want to marry Mr Kalin, but she thinks he'll look after me and Anoosheh. He won't, of course; he'll just get rid of us.

I won't let it happen, Padar, not while I'm the man of the house. The trouble is I'm not really a man yet. And this is not my house. I fear that if I can't find enough work to pay the rent and to feed us, Madar will decide she has no choice but to accept Mr Kalin's offer.

I hope some good will come our way soon. If it doesn't I'm not sure what we will do.

Naveed turns back into the alcove, to the rickety table with the jug and basin. Exhausted, he pours a little water into the basin and begins cleansing himself for the last prayer of the day – the Namaaz e Eshaa. He knows he is very late for the night prayer, but he had to finish the work on the Russian medals and badges while he still had the energy. Surely Allah will understand.

When the wud'u is finished Naveed stands up straight and takes a deep breath. With his hands raised to shoulder height, fingers slightly apart, he begins the first of the four raka'at, uttering his cry of faith.

'Allahu Akbar.'

Then he places both arms over his chest, right on top of the left, and goes on to prayer.

Chapter 11

'She's late again.'

Anoosheh stands with Naveed inside the school gate. They're waiting for her friend Pari.

'That's the fourth time this week.'

'Maybe she's decided to be like you,' says Naveed with a smirk. 'Always late, never ready, always keeping others waiting.'

'Very funny, big brother. Actually, I think you're the reason she's been late all this week.'

'Oh yes? And how can I be to blame?'

'All those eyes you've been making at her. I bet she's embarrassed.'

'Rubbish,' Naveed says, blushing.

'Don't think I haven't noticed. Everyone has.' Anoosheh's eyes glint with mischief. 'She's probably coming as late as possible in the hope that you won't be here to embarrass her more with those moony *I-love-you* looks you give her.'

'I don't!'

'You do.'

Naveed groans. 'Well, in that case I'll leave right now.'

'Don't be silly, brother.' Anoosheh grabs his arm. 'I'm only joking. In fact, if you must know, I think she likes you, too, though I can't imagine why.'

Anoosheh laughs as Naveed's face turns bright red. But then her brow furrows and her lips tighten.

'What is it?' Naveed asks.

'I'm not sure, but I think there is actually something wrong with Pari. I haven't seen her laugh once this week, and I've tried my best to make her. At lunchtime yesterday I thought she was about to cry. When I asked her what was wrong, she said it was nothing. When I kept asking, she snapped at me. Pari has never done that. *Never*.'

'I see.' Naveed sighs. 'We must—'

Before he can finish, Pari appears at the school gate. She is frowning and seems deep in thought. She falters as if unsure whether to enter. Anoosheh calls to her at once. A smile stamps itself on Pari's lips, but the frown stays, and the usual spring in her step is missing as she walks towards them.

'Good morning, Pari,' Naveed says. Her gaze is downcast and he suddenly realises that she is shaking. 'Pari? Are you all right?'

She looks up. Her eyes are red and puffed, with dark shadows under them.

'You've been crying.' Naveed says. 'What is the matter? Is there something we can do?' he asks as Anoosheh reaches out and takes her friend's hand.

Pari immediately pulls away; her smile vanishes and she stiffens.

'You are kind to be concerned,' she says, obviously struggling to control the tremble in her voice, her words clipped. 'But no, there is nothing you can do. Nothing at all.' She steps back and turns to Anoosheh. 'Sorry I'm so late. It's just tha—' She cuts herself off. 'Come along. We really should be in class.'

Without looking at Naveed again, Pari walks away with Anoosheh. All Anoosheh can do is glance back at him and shrug. He stares after them, wanting to call out to Pari, wanting to stop her, but knowing he cannot.

Once they have disappeared into the school building he slowly walks away, a lump in his throat.

Naveed crouches on a mountain of garbage, clutching his hessian bag, gazing out over a vast range of other mountains, piles left by the trucks that come and go. The waste disposal depot is huge, covering many acres several kilometres from Bagram Airfield. Naveed walked all the way this morning, but hopes he'll be lucky enough to hitch a ride back, especially since his bag is heavy. He's made some good finds today. Allah must be smiling on him. All he has to do now is keep hold of them, and that might not be so easy.

A convoy of trucks arrives. Naveed watches them dump their loads, beeping at the horde of children swarming around like rats in a feeding frenzy. One truck almost runs over a tiny girl who only just hobbles out of the way in time. None of the other children even notice this, though. They're too busy scurrying about, scavenging through the rubbish in a mad scramble, grabbing anything that might be of any value whatsoever, often fighting over items.

They have to move quickly, for a bulldozer squats to one side, a gnarled creature, growling impatiently. The moment the trucks drive away, it roars into action, herding the rubbish into mountains like the one Naveed is on. It rumbles relentlessly, blind to the hobblers, the weak or the slow. Even so, children keep flitting around it in a deadly dance, swooping perilously close to snatch things from the path of its heavy blade or bone-crushing tracks.

Naveed sees the mayhem, but knows that there is order behind it. Standing back, safely watching the little ones scrounge, is a group of older boys. Further away still are two men beside a battered Toyota pickup. The bonnet of the vehicle is raised, and the men have been working on the engine. Their main concern, though, is what happens with the rubbish, for they are the bosses of the depot gang, and everything happens according to their wishes.

When the garbage has been fussed and fought over and the best bits removed by the scavengers, the bigger boys step in and take a commission, basically whatever they want. The little ones know better than to argue. Then, before the next lot of trucks arrives, the older boys take their booty to the men in the Toyota, who sort through it and keep what they want. The boys are allowed to fight over what is left. And fight they do.

Naveed has no desire to be part of that mad scramble. He prefers to be a floater, sifting on his own through rubbish that has already been sifted through more than once by the depot gang. There are risks, of course. A few gang members might be sent to extract a fee from him, or some other lone forager stronger than he might muscle in. But Naveed is happy to take the risk. He keeps a low profile, mostly working out of sight of the gang, in the valleys between the mountains of garbage. It means he can move at his own pace, unhurried and unhassled. It also means he usually gets to keep what he gathers. He hopes that will be the case today because he's pleased with what he's found.

He inspects his collection of items. There are two music CDs, no doubt thrown out by US soldiers, and five cassettes of Afghan music. Tape spews from them, tangled and twisted, but Naveed is sure he can fix that. He has four glossy magazines as well, three in good condition, with pictures of Afghan film stars and singers. The three will sell well as they are, while he'll paste pictures from the damaged magazine onto cardboard sheets for jingle truck drivers to hang in their cabins.

And then there is the food. Naveed's eyes lit up when he saw the packets, seven of them, peeping from a buckled cardboard box. Sweet biscuits of some sort. Two packets had burst open and most of those biscuits were crushed and broken. But that didn't worry Naveed. He ate all the crushed ones without pausing, thanking Allah as he munched.

He licks his lips now, the memory of that sweetness still fresh in his mind as he gathers his gear and prepares to leave. He slides down from the top of the mound, careful not attract attention, and moves away. He follows the troughs between the piles of garbage, eventually emerging onto open ground a few hundred metres from the depot's exit. He can see the trucks lining up to leave. He can also see the Toyota with the two men and the boys standing around it, and he freezes at once, sensing danger.

The depot gang has finished dividing the load and is waiting for the next set of trucks to come. *Not good*, Naveed thinks, and slowly sinks to the ground. *They've got nothing to do; they're standing idle, gazing about. If they look my way I'm finished.* He edges towards the exit, keeping as low as he can.

There is only one truck still at the gate, the driver climbing up into his cabin. Naveed moves as quickly as he can in such a crouched position, covering half the distance to the exit. At this speed, though, he knows he will not make it before the truck drives away. He has no choice other than to stand up and sprint the last one hundred metres. It's a risk he has to take. But as soon as he straightens, one of the men sees him. He points and shouts. Immediately the gang turns as one and gives chase.

The boys are closer to the truck than Naveed, and they're not carrying a load as he is. There are some good lean runners among them. But Naveed has desperation on his side. If caught, he'll not only lose everything he's spent most of the day collecting. He'll be seriously bashed as a lesson. He's seen gangs like this one turn on a victim, and he doesn't want to be kicked and punched senseless.

So he runs as he's never run before, and manages to reach the truck a few metres ahead of the lead gang member. But the truck is accelerating, and run as he might, Naveed cannot quite catch it. He's exhausted, his legs are aching, his chest pounding, and he can hear the older boy right behind him, gaining by the second. It's no good, Naveed realises. He's not going to make it.

Drop the bag! a voice in his head yells as the truck draws away. *Save yourself. Drop it!*

At that moment Naveed sees the driver's face in the side mirror and screams out to him. The driver glances back and quickly sees what is happening. The truck slows down enough for Naveed to grab a bar across the tailgate. He hauls himself up just as the boy takes a running leap to tackle him. The truck accelerates away and the boy sprawls face first onto the gravel road.

Chapter 12

'I only just managed to hang on as the truck sped away. I could hear the whole gang yelling at me. Lucky they couldn't start their truck. Otherwise they'd have come after me.'

Naveed leans back and smiles at his mother and sister, laughing with a mix of relief and excitement. They've finished their evening meal, and it's been a good one. They've eaten well, far better than Naveed would have expected that morning. He's tired but contented, and delighted with how his day has gone.

'I still can't believe it,' he continues. 'Talk about good fortune! Once we were a safe distance from the garbage depot, the driver stopped and let me climb in with him. His name is Mr Omaid. He said I looked so desperate that he felt sorry for me and had to help. I am so glad he did.'

'We are too, my son,' says Naveed's mother. 'We owe Mr Omaid a debt of gratitude.'

'Yes, Madar. That is why I have asked him to share a

meal with us one night. Please don't be angry,' Naveed adds, on seeing her frown. 'I felt it was my duty. He saved me from a bad situation. And please don't worry about having a strange man in the house; he will be my guest, of course.'

'Of course. I understand, my son. You did the right thing. I'm more concerned about our home; it is so small and so—'

'Perhaps a picnic in the park, then. Whatever way, Mr Omaid is a humble man, Madar, and a kind one. He will not look down on us.'

'That is good, but what about food? Will we have enough? We can barely feed ourselves most of the time.'

'I will make sure we have enough, Madar. On my honour, I will not let us be shamed.' Naveed laughs and claps his hands. 'Stop your worrying. We've had a banquet tonight, have we not? We will again when Mr Omaid comes. I'll see to it.'

Naveed looks at the remainder of the meal still laid out before them. His mother made an excellent qorma, a lamb stew with caramelised onions, sultanas and spices, served with fluffy basmati rice baked in butter and salt. A big piece of nan is also left. They'll eat well for breakfast, too, he's pleased to see. And all thanks to his time at the waste disposal depot.

When Mr Omaid let him off in town he traded the two best cassettes of Afghan music and the one uncrushed packet of biscuits for the ingredients that went into this meal. It was extravagant, he knows, but he doesn't care. Seeing the smile on his mother's face, and hearing Anoosheh squeal with delight, has made it all more than worthwhile.

'God has definitely been watching over me today.'

'Perhaps,' says Anoosheh, shaking her finger at him like a scolding schoolteacher. 'But he may not watch over you next time.'

'There won't be a next time,' Naveed's mother says, her face turning serious. 'I forbid you to go to that horrible place.'

'But Madar, look at how well we have eaten tonight.'

'I don't care, Naveed. This is only one night.'

'There'll be more.'

'Not if you must risk your life for it, or even your health. Nothing is worth that. I mean it, my son. You know what those gangs can do. They could easily injure you so badly that you would never be able to work again. They could even kill you. What would your little sister and I do then, hmm?'

Naveed knows his mother is right. She and Anoosheh do need him.

'We would have nowhere to turn but Mr Kalin. You realise that, don't you?'

Her words send a chill right through Naveed. 'Of course, Madar,' he says at once. 'As you wish. I will not go back there.'

She leans across and kisses him on the forehead. 'We'd be lost without you, my son. Wouldn't we, daughter?'

Anoosheh nods and mumbles something. Her eyes are downcast, and Naveed notices that she is trembling slightly.

'Don't worry,' he assures her. 'I said I won't go back to the depot, and I mean it.'

Anoosheh remains staring at the floor, but shakes her head. 'I believe you, brother,' she mutters, almost swallowing the words. 'That's not the problem.'

Anoosheh has been quiet all afternoon. It's not like her. She didn't prattle and tease him on the way home from school. She didn't ask anything about his day, which she mostly would. She did brighten when he showed her the food he'd bartered for the cassettes and biscuits, and seemed happy enough as she helped prepare the evening meal. But her usual bubble and fizz were nowhere to be seen. And now she is all hunched up as if trying to hide from the world by becoming even smaller than she already is.

He reaches out and touches her. 'What is it, Noosh? What is the matter?'

She lifts her gaze from the floor and stares at him. Her big eyes are swimming in sadness.

'Madar's talk about Mr Kalin, that's what has upset me.'

'I'm sorry, little one,' her mother apologises. 'I only said it to make your brother see some sense in all this.'

'Yes, but it's true, Madar. That's what's so horrible about being a woman. Our lives are not our own. And that's not right. We're people, with hopes and dreams and feelings and everything that men have. And yet on our own we hardly even exist.'

Naveed and his mother glance at each other, neither knowing what to say.

'I used to be sad about having no legs,' Anoosheh continues. 'But now I realise it's a blessing in disguise. At least no man will ever want me; with no legs I'm no use to anyone.' She lets out a short laugh. 'Now I won't have to be married to some horrible man old enough to be my father, or even older.' She pauses, her voice faltering, her eyes welling with tears. 'Not like Pari. Poor, *poor* Pari.'

Naveed sits up at once. 'What do you mean?' he almost shouts.

'That's why she's been so sad lately. I kept at her today after you left us at school. In the end she broke down and told me: she is to be married.'

'Impossible,' Naveed says. 'She's so young!'

'Ha! That makes her even more marriageable, dear brother.'

'Who?'

'She doesn't know yet. But he'll be old, don't you worry. Her father has promised her to someone rich and important in payment of a debt he owes.'

'When?'

'Not for a while, but still too soon. She'll be married by the time winter returns.'

Naveed shudders at the thought. He sits in stunned silence, wishing there was something he could do but feeling a great weight of helplessness bearing down on him.

Later that night, after his mother and sister have gone to bed, Naveed works in the outside alcove on the goods he will have for sale at the market tomorrow. He's exhausted and his mind is a jumble of worries about Pari. But he has to make sure that everything is prepared. A great deal depends on it.

The items are lined up along the wooden bench, ready to be packed away in his hessian bag. The Russian medals and badges have been varnished, the cassettes and CDs cleaned, as have the saleable magazines. The broken biscuits have been repackaged in small plastic bags to sell separately. All the minor items are lined up as well – stationery, paperclips, pens and so on. And finally there are the Russian army shells – all cleaned and polished so they shine.

Naveed takes the biggest of these, an artillery shell approximately twelve centimetres in diameter and forty in height. It comes from a 122mm howitzer known as the D-30, one of the most lethal weapons in the Russians' armoury. It should sell well tomorrow.

He inspects the shell, pleased with how it sparkles, and then places it back on the bench. As he does so, his eyes fall on the medals, tags and badges. He glances back and forth between them and the big howitzer shell, and an idea shines in his mind.

'Yes,' he mutters excitedly. 'Not bad at all.'

Chapter 13

Naveed squats on his haunches and watches three soldiers make their way through the busy marketplace, a piece of cardboard held over his head for shade. The wind has dropped, and with it the choking dust, but the afternoon sun is still cruel. The soldiers must be very hot in their helmets and body armour, camouflage jackets, fatigues and heavy boots, he thinks. But they swagger through the crowd, pretending to be comfortable and relaxed, pausing at stalls and even trying to speak to people. He can tell they're on edge, though, their weapons at the ready.

A small cluster of children swarms about them like flies. A few stallholders and beggars call out as they pass. But most people either give them a wide berth or ignore them completely. The Americans believe such patrols win hearts and minds by giving some degree of security. But to many locals the soldiers are like aliens in their strange outfits: not wanted at best, fiercely hated at worst.

Naveed is pleased to see them, however. They mean business, and he needs more business. The day has not been as successful as he'd hoped. He'll make a small profit this time, after paying rent for his space, but that's all. There are only a couple of hours left before the market closes, and he was hoping for at least one more sale. Maybe these soldiers are it.

He stands, straightens his threadbare clothes and slicks down his hair. Then he rearranges his wares, making a single strategic change. He takes one particular item from the back, gives it a quick spit and polish and puts it in pride of place at the front of all the other things. That done, he sits cross-legged, his back straight, and looks up as the first of the soldiers draws level.

'Salaam alaikum, mister,' he says, raising his open palms to the soldier.

'Ditto, kid,' the American replies, busily chewing gum. He glances down at Naveed's wares and very nearly moves on. But then he sees what Naveed wants him to see.

'Hey, guys,' he calls to the others. 'Over here.'

Laid out on the black plastic is a strange assortment of items: three oranges, a bunch of plastic flowers, a number of neatly folded plastic bags, half a dozen sheets of once-white writing paper with odd envelopes, a few batteries, a pile of paperclips and a shoe box filled with second-hand cassettes and CDs.

Of course, none of these things interest the soldier. His attention has been caught by an artillery shell that sits among a number of smaller shells. The soldier swings his rifle to one side and leans down.

'That's Russian,' he says.

'Yes, mister,' Naveed replies, holding up the shell for the soldier to take. 'From Soviet gun. You know this?'

The American smiles and takes the shell.

'You bet I know this. It's from the D-30 howitzer. The Reds tried to blast you guys to hell and back with these. The place is riddled with the goddamn things.'

The soldier is right. D-30 shells are everywhere in Afghanistan, part of the military detritus the Russians left behind. So there is nothing unusual about this shell as such. It is what has been done to it that makes it special. It has been polished so that its casing shines, and Soviet medals, badges and military tags have been glued around the outside. Naveed did the job last night.

'Look at that, will ya?'

The soldier lowers his voice as he inspects the items adorning the shell. Each one would have been a thing of great personal value to the soldier who'd owned it. But they'd been abandoned like the tanks and guns and other equipment as the Soviets fled in panic.

'You guys really did kick ass back then. Did you make this?'

Naveed nods. 'Yes, I make. You like?'

'Yeah. It's cool. It's a kind of weird trophy.'

'Aha. You man of good taste.' Naveed claps his hands. 'We talk business, yes?'

The soldier laughs. 'And I see that you're a good

salesman. You'll go places, kid. And your English ain't half bad, neither.'

'Thank you, sir,' Naveed replies, and then waits patiently while the soldier further inspects the shell, turning it in his hand.

Eventually one of his mates gives him a shove.

'Come on, Horten. Just buy the freakin' thing and put the little guy out of his misery and let's go.'

'Yeah, of course.' The soldier holds up the shell. 'How much, kid?'

'What money you have? Afghani? Pakistan rupee? America dollar?'

The soldier pulls out a wad of Afghan money. He peels off a couple of notes without even looking and presses them into Naveed's hand. 'That do?'

Naveed is speechless. The soldier has given him far too much, ten times more than he would ever expect in his wildest dreams. He gapes at the money, struggling to contain his excitement; it is more than he would make in a whole month. He finds himself going over all the things he can buy for his mother and Anoosheh with so much money.

And yet, even as these thoughts tumble through Naveed's mind, he knows that he cannot keep the money. It would be wrong. It would be against everything his father stood for, and everything he hoped Naveed would in turn stand for.

Always try to be a good person, Naveed's father had said on many occasions. *Try to be the best person you possibly can. Try not to hurt others, or lie, or cheat, or steal. Those things are wrong. A tilted cart never reaches its destination.*

And Naveed knows exactly what his father would say now if he were still alive. He can hear him in his head.

The soldier does not know what he has given you. He does not know our money. To take it would be stealing. You must give it back.

But he is foolish, Padar, to have such money and not know its worth. A fool and his money . . .

Stealing is still stealing whether it be from a wise man or a fool. You must give it back.

Naveed wants to argue, but knows better. He looks up at the soldier, and holds out the money in the palm of his hand.

'What's the matter?' the soldier asks. 'Not enough?' He peels off another note. 'You drive a hard bargain, man.'

'No, no!' Naveed frantically shakes his head. 'Not more. You mistake. Is too much. Take back.'

'I don't believe it,' the soldier says to his mates. 'An honest Afghan.' They all laugh as Horten pushes away Naveed's hand. 'Listen, kid. I'm gonna be outta here in a couple of weeks, and your play money is worth exactly zilch back home. So take it. And here's another just for being honest. Go get yourself some decent shoes, huh.'

The soldier slaps him on the back and strides off with his mates.

Naveed watches them go, and then stares down at the money, barely able to believe his eyes. *Khoda ra Shuker, thank God!* This really is his lucky day. He feels like jumping and clapping and whooping and yelling all at once.

And he almost does. But then from the corner of his eye he sees that he's being watched. By them? The ones who watch everything? In his excitement he'd completely forgotten about them. Naveed breaks into a cold sweat.

How much did they see? he wonders. *Aram shoo*, he tells himself. *Calm down.*

He folds his hand around the four Afghan notes, squashing them into as small a ball as possible, and squats on his haunches again, trying to decide on his next move.

Chapter 14

Naveed packs his wares into the hessian bag. His movements are casual and unhurried, so as not to let on that he knows he's being watched. With his back turned, he peels and eats one of the oranges, and then chews on a piece of nan bread he's kept from the morning. At the same time he cups a small mirror in one hand and holds it up to check out who is spying on him.

Just as he thought. It's the Ranii boys; they're always snooping around the market on the lookout for easy money. They run a kind of protection racket; you pay them to leave you alone. They tried to make him pay earlier in the day, but he refused. Now they're back and he doubts they'll let him escape this time.

There are only three of them, though. The youngest and smallest member of the gang, the one they call The Flea, has his eyes fixed on Naveed, not letting him out of his sight. But the two older boys are busily glancing around, no doubt watching out for the rest of the gang.

Naveed considers making a run for it while they don't have the numbers. But before he can move, four more gang members turn up. A moment later their leader arrives as well, a thick-set youth about seventeen years old. He listens carefully to The Flea, glancing towards Naveed and nodding with a sneer as the small boy talks.

At that moment a trolley piled high with wares passes in front of the gang. Naveed seizes the opportunity. He grabs his bag, rolls to one side, and scrambles underneath a fruit and vegetable cart, almost upsetting it. The vendor shouts at him, but then quickly realises what is happening when he sees the gang members charging through the crowd, pushing people out of the way. He deftly kicks a few boxes in place to hide Naveed as the gang stops in front of his stall.

'Gom shoo!' he yells at them as they look about. 'Get lost.'

'The boy who's been there all day,' the gang leader snaps back, pointing to Naveed's selling place. 'Where did he go?'

The vendor waves his hand in the air. 'That way.' He points towards a narrow lane leading away from the marketplace. 'But you'll never catch him. He's too fast for you lazy donkeys. Go on, get out of here.'

The gang races off with other vendors cursing after them.

'Thank you so much, sir,' Naveed says, crawling from under the cart. 'I will repay you when I can.'

'Khwahesh mikonam – you're welcome,' the vendor replies. 'But hurry. God be with you.'

Naveed sprints away in the opposite direction to the gang. He is tempted to take a shortcut through the lanes and alleys, but decides to keep to the main road. It will take him longer to get home, but he feels safer in the open, surrounded by other people.

Once away from the marketplace, he relaxes a little and slows to a jog. The afternoon traffic is building up in both directions – soldiers returning to Bagram Airfield from their missions, merchants and workers heading home – but it is still moving quite quickly. Naveed makes good headway through the crowd, although he is barely aware of his surroundings; his mind is filled with the thrill of what happened that afternoon. He cannot believe his good fortune.

He is still holding the four notes tight in his clenched fist, longing to feast his eyes on them again. But he keeps moving, keen to place as much distance as possible between himself and the gang. Only when he is within a few hundred metres of the road that leads to Anoosheh's school does he allow himself a quick peep at the money.

He stops, opens his left hand a bit and peers down at the scrunched-up notes lying in his sweaty palm. He can hear his own heart thumping in his chest. This is more money than he has ever seen in his life. He folds the notes into his father's leather pouch and lets out a tiny squeal of delight. But a voice in the distance sends a chill of dread through his body.

'There he is!'

Naveed flicks his head around. A beaten-up black

utility is weaving in and out of the traffic, heading for him. Hanging off the back of it are the gang members. He curses and runs, pushing through pedestrians, carts and trolleys, darting into the very first lane he comes to, hoping it will be too narrow for the vehicle.

But it isn't. The utility screeches around the corner and races down the lane after him, scattering people before it. With the vehicle bearing down, Naveed just manages to slip into a thin alley on the right. The utility skids to a stop; the gang members leap off and charge down the alley after him, yelling and whooping like savages.

The lane twists and winds, becoming narrower all the time. Naveed has a good lead, but the gang is fresh and he can hear them gaining. They will catch him eventually, he thinks, and decides to get rid of the big money the American soldier gave him. While he runs he pulls the leather pouch over his head and then swiftly kneels and slips it into a hole at the base of a wall, shoving a piece of broken brick roughly into place to hide it.

He can hear their footsteps drawing closer; they are just out of sight, around the corner. Naveed forces himself to run on but it's not long before, exhausted, he decides to take the only course left to him. He stops at a very narrow part of the lane, turns and faces his pursuers. Gasping to catch his breath, he grabs a thick chunk of splintered timber from the gutter, raises it in the air and cracks the first of his pursuers over the head. The boy falls down, moaning, and the others stop on the spot.

There are seven of them, but they're bunched up in the narrow lane and no one is game enough to make the first move on Naveed. He half considers attacking them, but then the leader of the gang steps forward.

'Don't be stupid,' he says. 'You're outnumbered.'

'Maybe,' Naveed replies. 'But I'll take at least a couple of you down with me.' He raises the lump of wood over his shoulder as if to strike. The other members of the gang pull back, but the leader doesn't budge.

'You might, but we'll get you in the end, and you know it. Then we'll bash you real bad.' The gang leader grimaces. 'And I mean *real* bad.'

Naveed does know it, but doesn't flinch. 'In that case I'll have to make sure I bash as many of you as I can . . . *real* bad.'

'Or you could just give us the money and we'll leave you alone.'

Naveed thinks about this for a moment and then nods. 'Okay then.' Keeping his weapon raised, he pulls all the other money he made at the bazaar from his pocket. It amounts to about two hundred afghanis. 'Here you are.' He holds out the money but the leader shakes his head.

'Don't make me laugh. I mean the real money, the stuff the American gave you. The Flea reckons you got three big ones at least.'

'What?' Naveed exclaims. 'That's ridiculous. He's lying.'

'No. The Flea would never lie to me. He knows what I'd do to him if he did.' The leader glances down at the stunted little boy. 'Don't you?'

The Flea nods. 'The American gave him three big notes, maybe four, and at least two were for one thousand.'

'Are you crazy?' Naveed shouts. 'That soldier was as mean as they come. You were imagining things.'

'I saw it with my own eyes, boss,' The Flea insists. 'I did.'

'Impossible,' Naveed snaps. 'You must have been dreaming. '

'The Flea never misses anything,' the leader adds with growing impatience. 'His eyes are as sharp as a hawk's. I'm tired of being nice. The money, hand it over. Now.'

'But I don't—'

Before Naveed can utter another word, the leader snaps his fingers and the gang springs forward. He lashes out with his club, striking two of them, but then the rest are all over him like a single beast. He tries to fight back, but the piece of wood is ripped from his hands and he's knocked to the ground under a rain of blows – kicking, punching, stamping, thumping. He curls up in a tight ball and prepares for the worst. A boot wallops into his back, another crashes down on his shoulder, and he screams with agony.

But then the beating suddenly stops. One moment the gang members are all over him; seconds later they are scrambling off, yelling and falling over each other to get away. Naveed rolls sideways to see a yellowy-white flash. It's the dog. She bounds over the top of him, snarling and snapping ferociously at the gang.

73

The leader hurls the lump of wood at her, but she dodges it and leaps straight onto him, snapping at his face. He stumbles back and falls with a heavy thud, the dog landing on top. He screams for the others to help, but they've already fled, leaving him to his fate. He tries to struggle to his feet, but the dog has him pinned to the ground, about to tear a piece out of his neck.

Naveed gapes in horror. She might kill him.

'No!' he yells, leaping up. 'Stop!'

The dog does as she's told. She still has her mouth open, her sharp teeth poised to strike, a low growl rumbling in her throat. But she pulls back slightly, and looks as though she's waiting for Naveed's next command.

'Get the dog off me,' the gang leader begs, blubbering like a baby, his face gashed and bloody. 'Please.'

Not quite sure what to do, Naveed calls gently to the hound. 'Here, girl,' he says, patting the side of his leg. 'Let him go. Come here to me.'

After a slight pause, the dog seems to relax a little. She closes her massive jaw, stops growling, and steps off the gang leader, still keeping her eyes fixed on him as she backs away. He immediately scrambles to his feet and runs for his life.

Naveed stands in the narrow lane as the escaping footsteps fade, a tiny smile trickling across his face and turning into a great big grin. He laughs out loud, barely able to believe his good fortune. The dog is next to him, staring up with a curious expression, her head cocked to one side.

'You've just found yourself a home,' he says. 'And I've just found myself a friend for life.'

He kneels down and wraps his arms around her in a big hug. 'Thank you,' he whispers, barely able to hold back the tears of gratitude. He has no doubt that the gang could easily have killed him without a second thought, especially if they couldn't find the money. They would certainly have left him seriously injured. 'Thank you so much.'

Chapter 15

Life's good.

Naveed can't stop smiling. He's been smiling for the good part of a week, ever since that day at the bazaar. He spent the first two days on his back, recovering from the ordeal. His wounds and bruises have largely healed now, although he has a gash on his forehead that will take some time to mend. And his body still aches from the pummelling it received. But inside he feels wonderful.

He reaches out and pats the dog sitting beside him. The dog? *His* dog. His saviour! He's called her Nasera – *she is beautiful like the moon* – because her yellowy-white coat and broad face make her look like a piece of the moon. She gazes up at him now with her big moony face, and seems to be smiling too.

Naveed is with his mother and sister in a park on the northern side of town. They're sitting under a tree, quietly eating sheer yakh, ice-cream sprinkled with pistachios, each of them lost in their thoughts. Even Anoosheh is silent for a change. She chatted all morning while they were shopping, but is now savouring every bite of her frozen treat. So is his mother, as she gazes at a flock of colourful kites fluttering in the sky on the other side of the park.

It took his mother a while to get over the shock of seeing him arrive home from the market that afternoon, Anoosheh leading him like a blind man, a ghostlike mastiff trailing close behind. He was a mess, limping badly, covered in blood, lips swollen, eyes puffed and bruised.

'Ayee, my son!' she screamed. 'In Allah's name, what has happened?'

'Don't worry, Madar,' he croaked. 'Everything is good. We're rich.' He chuckled, coughed up a little blood, and promptly collapsed.

And they *were* rich, at least compared to before. The money the American soldier gave Naveed for the artillery shell would look after food and rent for months. It didn't mean they could be extravagant, but it did mean that the stress of their daily hand-to-mouth existence had gone for the time being. Life had smiled on them for a change.

It meant they could afford a few luxuries at last. Naveed could get that new toshak he'd promised himself. They could buy a rug for the cold earthen floor, and maybe even a bukhari for heating. The pleasure alone of going shopping together could be theirs, a luxury in itself.

That's what they've been doing all morning, first at the market for food, and later at Mr Waleed's for those special things. Naveed is looking forward to sleeping on the new toshak he has just bought. Their mother also purchased materials to make Anoosheh a dress. And for herself she bought a headscarf. She wore it out of the shop. Made of mauve chiffon, it suited her so well that Mr Waleed couldn't help telling Naveed how beautiful his mother was.

Gazing across at her now, Naveed can only agree with the shopkeeper; she is indeed beautiful. But far more important than that, he thinks to himself, is her strength as a person – inside, where it matters.

Naveed's mother has chosen not to wear the burqa, although many women do. She continues to wear a simple head-covering such as a scarf when in public, and Naveed knows how difficult this has made things for her sometimes. It has meant that she's not gone out as much as she'd like. It's meant that men have stared at her in unpleasant ways, and some have even made comments. Once when accompanying her he wanted to confront these men. But she stopped him.

'Ignore them, my son. They are such little men,' she said, holding her head high and proud.

How proud she looks now, he thinks, a shaft of afternoon sun highlighting her face with its soft glow.

'Why are you staring at me like that?' she asks, interrupting his thoughts.

He blushes. 'Sorry, Madar. I was only thinking—'

'That we should have bought a kite!' Anoosheh breaks in, pointing with her spoon to the kites across the park. Several teams are practising in preparation for

78

a big competition to be held in the park in a couple of days. 'I could have entered the tournament,' she says, 'and become a champion kite flyer!'

'You'll have enough to do helping me look after Naveed's guest,' her mother replies. 'He has asked Mr Omaid to join him here to have a picnic and watch the competition.'

'A picnic? Can I bring Pari as well?'

'Of course you can, if her parents agree.'

As his sister and mother talk, Naveed's eyes rest on Nasera. He's pleased to see how much her condition has improved in barely a week. But then he has fed her well, arranging to take any food scraps from the back of Mr Waleed's shop. He's also found her a basket and a thick old rug to sleep on in the alcove at the front door of their house. She has made herself quite at home there.

She's made herself part of the family, too, adopting the three of them without a second thought, along with a grubby little ragdoll she found in the lane behind Mr Waleed's shop when Naveed was collecting scraps. The doll is old and worn. An arm and a foot were missing, and the stuffing was falling out until Anoosheh sewed on new parts and added more filling. Nasera now treats the thing as her own, like a baby, keeping it in her bed and curling up with it at night.

Naveed shakes his head in disbelief as he gazes down at Nasera. He cannot get over how lucky he is that this special dog seems to have chosen him to be part of her life, to put her trust in. No wonder he can't stop smiling.

Life really is good.

He peeps into the bag that holds their purchases, and chuckles. 'Time to go home,' he tells his mother and sister. 'I think I'm ready to try out my new toshak!'

Chapter 16

'No doubt about it, bud,' the American commander tells Jake as they climb out of their Humvee at the entry control point into Bagram Airfield. 'Your dog saved some lives today.' The other soldiers from the Humvee grunt in agreement.

They've been on an early morning mission to a mountain village known to harbour Taliban. Stingray sniffed out a pile of explosives, enough to blow a whole town sky high. He also located an IED on the roadside when they were leaving the village.

'That was big,' the commander says. 'We'd have lost guys for sure.' He pats Stingray. 'You can come on an op with me any day, boy.' Then he turns to Jake. 'Join us for a drink?'

'Thanks, but I might take Stingray for a quick walk into town and back.' When the commander frowns, Jake continues, 'I really need to get him more used to being around people. He's still a tad uneasy with them.'

The commander shrugs. 'Okay then, if you must. But be careful, huh?'

'Don't worry, I've got good company.' Jake pats his M16.

'There's some kind of kite comp on today, you know,' the commander adds. 'They've been building up to it all week. So there'll be a crowd. They sure love their kites here.'

'So do I, as a matter of fact,' Jake replies with a grin. 'Used to fly them as a kid.' He gives the commander the thumbs up. 'Back soon.'

Jake clips the leash onto his dog. It's a beautiful early spring Saturday, the sun high in a kerosene sky. A moderate breeze sweeps in, tinged with aromas of cooking. Jake hears a fluttering sound and looks up. The sky in the distance is alive with kites. The sight puts a smile on his face.

'Come on, Stingers. Let's check 'em out.'

❖❖❖

'I told you we should have put in a team,' shouts Anoosheh, keenly watching the kite-flying competition. 'I would have been the pilot, of course. You, brother, would make a passable runner.'

'How come I only get to be number two?'

'Many reasons, brother dear. Skill, for a start. I'd make a far better kite flyer than you. And then there's killer instinct. Sorry, but I fear you don't have what it takes in that area.'

She thumps Naveed on the arm as they watch the kites fight it out in the sky above them, swooping and diving, trying to cut each other's strings with their razor-sharp edges.

Naveed looks about and nods happily to himself. A picnic on a beautiful day, delicious smells from food stalls filling the air, the sky alive with a clutter of kites, people out and about enjoying themselves. What could be better? These are the good things in life.

Mr Omaid is with them for the picnic. He is guest of honour, and sits in a special place with Naveed, attended to by Anoosheh and her mother, who sit apart from the males. Pari is there as well. She is laughing with Anoosheh; how Naveed loves seeing Pari laugh.

And a little distance away is Nasera. Naveed gazes fondly at his canine friend. She sits to attention – on her haunches, back straight – as though guarding the family, the stamp of nobility in her bearing.

He notices that people tend to give Nasera a wide berth as they walk past. Some even stare disapprovingly at her. Naveed is not surprised – many Afghans dislike dogs – but their disapproval means nothing to him. Nasera saved his life, and he will never forget it.

'See,' Anoosheh says to Pari. 'My brother is not even watching the contest. He has eyes only for that dog of his. I don't think I'll make him my runner after all. Pari, you can have the job; you'll be much better at it. What do you say? Next year you and I will show up the boys.'

Pari laughs at this, but Naveed catches just a glimpse of sadness in her eyes. Next year she will probably be married to a man old enough to be her father, perhaps older. He wishes there was something he could do or even say to ease her pain. He is about to speak when Nasera suddenly growls and stands up on all fours, the hair bristling down her back.

'What is it?' Naveed asks, looking around.

'Amrikai,' Mr Omaid says. 'American.' He points across the park. 'And he has a dog.'

Naveed stares for a moment and smiles. 'I know him. He is a good man. He is the one who gave us the chocolate bars, Madar.' He scrambles to his feet. 'I'll be back in a minute,' he says, and sets off across the park.

'Mr Jake,' he yells as he runs, Nasera loping along close behind.

Jake doesn't hear Naveed. He's busy patting Stingray. He is pleased with how the kelpie has been handling the crowd, but the strange whirring, squealing and fluttering of the kites is still making him a little on edge.

'Good boy.' Jake takes the ball from his pocket and tosses it in the air. Stingray leaps up and catches it. 'You've done real good, mate. We might call it a day, eh?'

Jake is about to turn around. But Stingray's whole body tenses. He drops the ball and springs forward, straining at the leash, almost pulling free.

Chapter 17

'Mr Jake. Hello, Mr Jake.'

Jake recognises Naveed and waves. But then he sees the mastiff lolloping behind, and freezes. It's a big dog, bigger than Stingray, and quite possibly aggressive; a lot of Afghan dogs are. The very last thing he wants is for a fight to break out between them. Jake knows he can control Stingray, but can the boy control his dog? With Naveed about twenty metres away, Jake holds up his hand.

'Stop!' he commands in a firm voice. 'Stop right there.'

Naveed instantly does as he's told, but Nasera keeps going, straight past him.

'Your dog!' Jake shouts. 'Call it back. Now!'

Naveed sees the concern on Jake's face and yells at once. 'Nasera. Stop.' But the dog keeps running. 'Nasera!'

Jake prepares for the worst, pulling Stingray to his side. But to his amazement the big hound stops on

Naveed's second command, no more than ten metres away. Jake sighs with relief and relaxes a little.

'Sorry, Mr Jake,' Naveed calls when he catches up to Nasera. 'I not mean trouble for you.'

'No worries,' Jake replies. 'I'm impressed already. You've got good control of your dog. All the same, I'd be happier if you put this on her before you come any closer.' He pulls out the belt from around his waist and tosses it to Naveed. 'Just in case.'

Naveed secures the belt around Nasera's neck and takes a firm grip of it.

'Great,' says Jake. 'Now hold her tight and walk this way, nice and slow.'

Again Naveed does as he's told, and Nasera keeps right by his side.

Jake watches the pair closely. 'Excellent,' he says, nodding his head approvingly. When they're about two metres away he raises his hand again. 'That's close enough.' Naveed stops. 'So far so good. Now comes the tricky bit. Keep a good hold on your dog. Okay?'

'Yes, Mr Jake. I hold good.'

Jake slowly edges forward in short steps, gradually closing the gap between them, both dogs making little whining noises that grow louder the closer they get to each other.

'Right,' Jake says when they're less than a metre apart. 'Time for our dogs to meet. You keep yours there and I'll let mine approach.'

Stingray is really tugging on his leash now, but strangely enough Nasera is not, much to Naveed's relief;

he doubts he could hold her back if she really did pull hard. Instead she stands erect and alert, looking quite regal, her stare fixed on the other dog as his master allows him to creep closer.

It is a tense moment for Jake and Naveed as the dogs come nose to nose and begin smelling each other. The tension grows as Stingray is allowed to move along Nasera's side, both dogs sniffing intently, their tails stiff, the hair standing up along their backs. But then, when they've eventually nosed each other all over, they both start wagging their tails.

'Well I never,' Jake says, shaking his head. 'I haven't seen anything like that before. Instant friends. It's amazing.' He offers his hand to Naveed. 'Congratulations, and good to see you again.' They shake, Naveed beaming with pride.

'Mr Jake, please,' he says. 'I want you meet my family. This way, I beg you.'

Jake doesn't want to stay away from the base for too much longer, but he also doesn't want to offend his young friend.

'With pleasure,' he replies and follows Naveed.

As they cross the park, Jake cannot help but notice a definite change in Stingray. The dog has become completely calm and relaxed, not at all nervous of the noises around him now. He's perfectly happy to pace along beside Nasera, his ball in his mouth. And when they reach Naveed's family, Stingray simply sits to one side with Nasera, as though they've known each other forever. Jake is delighted.

'Please, my good friend,' Naveed says to Jake.

He is beaming more than ever, his white teeth sparkling. Lined up behind him are several people – a woman and two girls, and a man standing slightly apart.

'My mother,' Naveed continues, touching the woman lightly, the affection unmistakable in his voice. 'She is glue of family. Without her we nothing.'

The woman nods to Jake and then lowers her gaze.

'My little sister Anoosheh.'

The smaller of the two girls stands partly behind her mother, but Jake can see that she's on crutches. When she hobbles forward he catches his breath.

'Thank you, brother,' she says, grinning cheekily at Naveed. 'I only *little* sister because someone stole my legs.' She turns her smile on Jake, who laughs.

'And this Pari,' Naveed says, ignoring his sister. 'Friend of Anoosheh.'

Pari dips her head respectfully at Jake, smiles briefly and turns her eyes to the ground.

'And this,' Naveed continues, introducing Mr Omaid. 'Very kind man who look after me when I have trouble. Mr Omaid.'

'Salaam alaikum,' Mr Omaid says.

'Wa alaikum as-salaam,' Jake replies, hoping he's said it the right way. 'To all of you.'

Jake looks around at these people – the boy he met in the minefield, and his family and friends – and feels drawn to them, in much the same way that Stingray seems drawn to the boy's dog. There is something soft and gentle, warm and friendly and real about them. He knows he can't stay away from the base for much longer without his absence causing alarm. But when he's asked to join them for chai he really cannot say no.

The mother and the man say very little, either from modesty or lack of English, or both; Jake can't tell. But Naveed's sister talks enough for all of them, waving her hands around to illustrate her point when she cannot find the English words.

'Your English is very good,' Jake says to Anoosheh. 'Do they teach it at school?'

'Yes, Mr Farzin say I am top English student,' Anoosheh replies. 'Unless Naveed come back,' she adds, smiling at her brother.

'You don't go to school, mate?' Jake asks Naveed.

Naveed hesitates, then shakes his head. 'Not possible,' he says.

'He must work,' Anoosheh explains. 'He man of house.' She pauses briefly to let Jake take this in, and then adds: 'Our father died from suicide bomber.'

Jake is stunned, not just by what she said but how she said it: so matter-of-fact for someone so young.

'Bloody hell,' he gasps under his breath. 'That's terrible.'

'Yes, Mr Jake,' Naveed says quietly. 'Is terrible. But Padar still with us. In here, you see?' He taps his chest.

'Yeah,' Jake replies in a whisper, struggling for words. 'I do see.'

He doesn't want to leave now. But he's been away from the base far too long. He'd hate them to send out a search party. Jake stands and thanks Naveed's mother for her hospitality. Then he turns to Stingray, and notices at once that Nasera now has the ball. Not only that, but she is constantly picking it up and dropping it at Naveed's feet. The boy is ignoring her, but she keeps it up.

'Hey, does she often do that?' Jake asks Naveed.

'I not sure. We not together much time, but I know she good dog. She save my life.'

'Yeah? Well, I think she might be able to save other lives as well.'

'What you mean?'

'There isn't time to explain now. But could you bring her to Bagram Airfield tomorrow morning, first thing?'

'Yes, I can do.'

'You will come, won't you? I mean, for sure.'

'Sure, I come. Word of honour. First thing in morning.' Naveed holds out his hand.

'Good, mate.' Jake shakes it vigorously. 'Bloody good!'

Chapter 18

'I would like to pay an extra month in advance, if you will permit it, sir.'

Naveed kneels on the floor in front of Mr Kalin, a large man who wheezes and shifts uncomfortably under his own weight from time to time. He takes up most of the mat on which he sits, lounging back on the few cushions that Naveed's mother has arranged to make him as comfortable as she can in her simple home. He sips chai through a sugar cube held between his teeth as he considers Naveed's request, and munches on a mix of nuts and raisins. Naveed's mother and sister sit in the corner to one side.

Mr Kalin is dressed to show his wealth and position. His pale grey perahan toombon is made of expensive wool, over which he wears a shiny emerald-green chapan with dark purple stripes. The purple dismal around his neck is woven through with silver thread. He has gold on both wrists – a bracelet on one, a solid watch on the other. A thick gold chain hangs around his neck.

He glances about the room, turning up his nose at the cramped space, but secretly impressed by how neat and clean it is. Clearly this woman is a good housekeeper, a factor in her favour, he decides.

'I see,' he replies eventually. 'A month in advance, eh? You must be rich.'

'Oh no,' Naveed laughs. 'Far from it, kind sir. But Allah has seen fit to place some work in my path each day. And I have learned from your wise example to save carefully and pay for the things that must be paid for first. We eat next, and if there's anything left—' He stops and shrugs. 'But then there hardly ever is.'

'Very sensible, my boy. Perhaps I may allow you to work for me one day when you're older.'

'That would be too much of an honour,' Naveed lies, half-expecting his sister to snicker. He has often told her how much he would hate working for Mr Kalin. The man is known to be a mean employer.

Mr Kalin toys with the gold chain around his neck. 'My business is expanding every day, exceeding my own expectations. Why only last week I had to rent yet another warehouse to store the items I'm bringing in from Pakistan. Who knows, one day I might even be as rich as you, young man!'

He laughs uproariously and takes the rent money, checking the notes before folding and pocketing them.

'In fact, business is so good that my friends tell me I should seriously consider taking a third wife.' He turns his gaze slightly towards Naveed's mother.

A tense silence fills the little room. Naveed has been

dreading this moment, his mother even more, both convinced that the visit was always about more than just collecting the rent. As they struggle to think of a reply, the tension builds, punctuated by Mr Kalin's wheezing.

It is Anoosheh who saves the day. Without warning she breaks into a fit of violent coughing.

'Forgive me,' she splutters between coughs.

'What is it?' Mr Kalin says, edging away. 'What's the matter with her?'

Naveed catches the tiniest wink from his sister's eye. 'I'm sorry,' he says to Mr Kalin. 'I didn't want to trouble you with Anoosheh's illness. It is our concern, not yours, sir.'

'Illness? Is it contagious?' Mr Kalin brings his scarf to his face.

'I don't think so. Although now you ask, my mother and I have not been feeling all that well of late.' Naveed shakes his finger at Anoosheh. 'Cover your mouth, girl.' He then grabs the teapot. 'Pay no attention to her, kind sir. It will pass soon. Some more chai, perhaps?'

Mr Kalin cannot dismiss Naveed's offer quickly enough. He clicks his fingers and a bodyguard immediately rushes in from the outside alcove, helping him to his feet. Mr Kalin hauls his bulk across the room as rapidly as he can, Anoosheh's coughing fit growing worse all the time. He completely ignores Naveed's mother, who stands with her head bowed, bidding farewell, and hurries through the doorway, muttering to Naveed from behind his scarf.

'Outside, boy. A word.'

Naveed follows, struggling to keep a straight face. Out in the street, Mr Kalin glares at him.

'You should have told me. I would never have entered if you had.'

'I really am sorry, sir, but I thought Anoosheh was better. She hasn't coughed like that for many days. I'm sure it is nothing. I'm sure you will be fine.'

'I hope so, for your sake as much as mine.' Mr Kalin lowers the scarf from his face. 'There are two other matters, though.' He glances towards Nasera; she sits just inside the alcove, her eyes fixed on him.

'First of all, that dog. I'm not sure I should let you keep it.'

'You will never find a better guard dog, sir. Only the other night she chased away a gang that was lurking around your warehouse.'

'Is that so? But is she trustworthy? She looks like she might bite at any minute.'

'Only thieves and anyone who might want to hurt her.' Naveed can tell that Nasera doesn't like Mr Kalin; the curl in her lip that twitches as she stares at him from the alcove is the start of a snarl. 'But you needn't worry, sir. It's easy to see that she likes you. See that curl in her lip? She's smiling at you.'

Mr Kalin is not completely convinced of this. But he likes the idea that his warehouses might be safer. 'A guard dog, eh?'

'The best.'

'Very well, then, you can keep her for now. But don't let her get in my way.'

'Of course not, Mr Kalin.' Naveed dips his head in respect. 'And the other matter?'

'Ah, yes. In the park today.' Mr Kalin stares Naveed straight in the eye. 'You were seen being very friendly to an American soldier.'

'I think he is Australian. And I don't really think he is a soldier.'

'Don't mince words with me, boy. He's a foreigner and he was seen sitting with you, talking, laughing, taking chai. Explain yourself.'

Naveed has to think quickly.

'Whoever told you this is not only malicious but a poor spy. If they had bothered to look closely they would have seen that the man was not interested in me, but in my dog. He wanted to buy it, that's all. He said he knew a good guard dog when he saw one, and tried to persuade me to sell. I refused, of course, but we had to be courteous to him. That is the Afghan way, surely, sir.'

'Yes, yes, I suppose so. As long as that's all there was to it. But remember this. No matter how friendly he might have been, he is still a foreigner, one of the invaders. Everyone at that air base is. We don't want them here. Take from them, by all means. Accept their money, but never their friendship. They are leaving, as you know, just as the Russians left, and those before them. And when they've gone, those who befriended them will pay the price.'

Mr Kalin slices his finger across his neck like a knife, and without another word walks away.

Naveed watches him go, a shudder running right through him. A moment later he feels Nasera rub against him, her muzzle nudging at his hand. She has the ragdoll held gently in her huge jaws. He kneels and hugs her close.

When Naveed enters the house, his mother and sister are squatting on the floor in each other's arms, their eyes wet from laughing. They stare at him for a moment and then all three burst into laughter.

Chapter 19

When Naveed and Nasera arrive at Bagram Airfield the next morning, Jake is called, and soon joins them, Stingray at his side. The two dogs immediately recognise each other, and after a round of sniffing and piddling are happy to trot along like old friends as Jake leads the way through the base.

'This place is just like an American town,' he explains. They are walking along Disney Drive, the main street on the base. Signs point everywhere. 'It's in sections like suburbs. There are even traffic lights, and they have peak hours.'

Naveed is enthralled. He knows the base is enormous, even though he's never actually been in it before. But he cannot get over the size of the place, the endless activity, the mass of troops and personnel, the many vehicles moving about, the vast fleet of aircraft, and the constant humming and drumming.

There seem to be shops everywhere as well, some with big bright signs. Naveed manages to read a few –

Burger King, Dairy Queen, Supermarket – but others are beyond him.

'All these places are here to make the soldiers feel at home,' Jake explains. 'Why, there are gyms and cinemas, and even a beauty salon.'

At least there is also a little bit of Afghanistan inside the base, Naveed notices, as they pass a string of stores run by Afghan merchants selling rugs, carpets, craft and jewellery. And he's pleased to see the brightly painted jingle trucks, too, which help with construction work about the base. But despite these familiar sights and sounds, Naveed feels as though he has stepped into another world, one far removed from his own.

The strange thing is that Nasera seems perfectly at home. Naveed was worried that the base might frighten her. But it hasn't at all. She simply wanders along next to Stingray as if she's always been part of the scenery.

They go out to the far side of Bagram Airfield, well away from the main accommodation and service area. Here Jake puts Stingray through some exercises and then runs a series of tests on Nasera.

He throws balls for the dogs to chase and retrieve, hiding and burying things for Stingray to find, all the while noting what Nasera does and how she reacts. He makes different sorts of loud noises around the dogs, banging tins, shouting and firing guns into the air. Naveed is not sure what it's all about, for Jake has been too engrossed to explain. But for the moment he's happy just to watch and wonder what the Australian is up to.

Eventually, after a couple of hours, Jake stops the exercises and turns to Naveed.

'It's as I thought yesterday, in the park. She's a natural.' He shakes his head in amazement. 'I thought I might have been imagining things, but no. In fact I'd go so far as to say she's even better than I expected.'

Naveed frowns. 'Please, Mr Jake,' he says. 'What you mean, Nasera *a natural*?'

'Yeah, I'm sorry. I just needed to check her out on a few points before I said anything to you. But I can tell you now that Nasera has the makings of a top arms and explosives search dog. As far as I can see, she has all the right qualities. She's got an excellent sense of smell, she's a great retriever, she's very obedient and keen to please, and she doesn't seem at all upset by loud noises. I've never seen a dog more relaxed around Bagram base; it took Stingray weeks to settle down here, and even now a really loud explosion will upset him. The bottom line is your dog is amazing.'

'Thank you, Mr Jake, but I still not sure what you want.'

'We run a program, training dogs to detect land-mines, IEDs, hidden explosives and weapons. It's all part of the fight against terrorists. We need good dogs like Nasera.'

'Aha, I see. You want Nasera?'

'That's right.'

'Not possible.' Naveed shakes his head. 'Sorry, but she stay with me. She—'

'No, Naveed, I'm not asking you to part with her. I'd like you to be in the program as well, as Nasera's handler.'

'Me? You want me do job like you?'

'Too right I do.'

'But I not know how.'

'Not true, mate. I said Nasera was a natural. But so are you. I've watched you both – you're a team. It takes months to get that kind of bond between a dog and its handler – you've got it already. The rest we can teach you. You're both fast learners.'

'But, Mr Jake, I just a boy.'

'Yeah, well, that could be a spanner in the works with the bosses. But I know how to pull a few strings around here, and as far as I'm concerned you're not just a boy at all, at least not where it matters.' Jake points to his head. 'Not up here.' Then he points to Naveed's chest. 'And not in there, either.' He rests his hand on Naveed's shoulder. 'Listen, I don't want to push you into anything. Just say you'll think about it, eh?'

Naveed doesn't have to think about it. He knows the answer already – yes, yes and yes. He wants to shout it. But just getting the word past his lips is far more difficult than he realised. There's a lump in his throat getting in the way.

'What's the matter?' Jake frowns. 'Have I upset you?'

'No, Mr Jake,' Naveed says. 'I happy. I seeing some light.'

Jake smiles. 'So is that a yes?'

Naveed laughs. 'Yes, is yes!'

Jake beams back at him. 'Excellent. We start tomorrow, then. Okay with you?'

Naveed nods.

'Oh, there is one other thing,' Jake adds. 'I'm thinking Nasera must have a toy of some sort. You know, something cuddly that she carts around or plays with or takes to bed. Am I right?'

'Yes,' Naveed replies. 'She got old doll. How you know?'

'Just a hunch. Make sure you bring it with you tomorrow.'

'Why bring?'

'You'll see.'

❖❖❖

After Naveed leaves, Jake reports to his boss about his session.

'I see it like this, Joe. The dog's good, the boy's good, and I'm good to go.'

'You don't think he's a bit young? I mean it's hard enough getting adults to stick with a serious training program. How do you know the kid won't just walk out halfway through?'

'I don't. But I'm willing to bet he won't. And I really believe we can do some good here.'

'Okay then. You don't have any missions scheduled for the next week. So go ahead. Give him and the dog a few hours each day. By the end of the week you'll know if you've got a goer or not.'

'Thanks.' Jake turns to leave. At the door he pauses. 'Oh, there is one other thing,' he says. 'Artificial arms and legs? What do you call those things?'

'Prosthetics?'

'Yeah, that's it. They do them at the hospital here on the base, don't they?'

'Sure. There's a special unit. Why?'

'Who's the best person to see?'

'Doctor Radcliffe. She's as busy as all hell, but tell her I sent you.'

'Thanks again.' Jake disappears through the doorway.

'Hey. You haven't answered me. Why?'

'Another time, Joe,' Jake calls over his shoulder.

Chapter 20

Naveed's mother and sister have long since gone to bed, but he is wide awake. Although it must be after midnight he is still bubbling with excitement from the events of the day, thoughts racing through his mind. He has left the little room where they live and sits just inside the alcove. Nasera lies beside him, her head resting on his leg, her eyes on her ragdoll, which she has dropped in his lap. He gazes down the narrow lane that runs past the house, and then up at the sky strewn with jewel-like stars. A fog is drifting in.

He can hear the big carrier planes still taking off and landing at Bagram Airfield. This is the best time for them to do that, safer from attack than in daylight. Even so, a flare flickers into the night accompanied by mortar blasts to the east: definitely Taliban. A chorus of gunfire chatters in reply, followed by a mighty explosion that makes the ground shudder and lights up the sky. A quiet period follows – dogs bark, a cat yowls, someone shouts something somewhere.

Earlier that night, Naveed didn't say much to his mother or sister about his time at the base with Jake, despite their many questions. One part of him desperately wanted to tell everything. But caution made him hold back; if nothing came of it, the disappointment would be so great for all of them. And if something did eventuate, the joy would be so much greater. 'Don't expect anything,' he said with a shrug over their evening meal. 'But I'll go back for a few days just in case. Who knows?'

'Just imagine,' he now whispers to Nasera. 'We could save people, save lives, limbs.' With that thought alone, life has suddenly taken on an extra meaning for Naveed. It doesn't have to be only about getting up and finding work in order to eat. It can be about much more.

When he was at the base, Naveed couldn't explain to Jake why he'd become so emotional. At the time he wasn't even sure himself. Now he knows that a great weight has been lifted from him. And with that weight has gone some of the darkness that has filled his life ever since Anoosheh lost her legs, made even more intense when his father died.

For years he'd carried the darkness wherever he went, never letting on to anyone, especially his mother and sister, always showing a brave face. He had to; he was the man of the house. But in fact it had been slowly eating away at him.

Now it has lifted a little, at least enough for him to see ahead. Never has anything so wonderful happened to him. This is a chance to end the darkness forever.

Naveed knows he has to grasp it with both hands – no, more than that – with all his heart and soul.

'I'll do it, Padar,' he whispers. 'You'll be proud of me.'

Nasera looks up at him, her head cocked sideways, and makes a whining noise.

'Bebakhshid – sorry,' he says to her. 'I meant you, too. *We* will do it; that's what I really meant.'

He gives her an extra big hug. But she growls and pulls away, leaping up.

'What's the matter?'

Nasera's ears are pricked, her eyes alert as she listens intently. She sniffs at the air and growls again. Naveed can hear something as well now – muted voices at the far end of the lane. He catches a whiff of diesel fumes.

'Quiet,' he whispers to her, and carefully gets to his feet.

Something feels wrong. There is hardly ever any night-time activity in this area. It's a storage district, mainly filled with warehouses. Naveed and his family are the only people actually living in the lane. There's plenty of action through the day, trucks and people from before sunrise into the early evening. But never as late as this.

'Come.' Naveed beckons to Nasera. He tosses the doll into her bed and creeps down the laneway, keeping flush with the wall.

The voices grow louder as Naveed approaches the parking area for Mr Kalin's warehouse, about halfway down the lane. The voices are still too muffled for him to hear exactly what's being said, but he does recognise one, that of Mr Kalin, and peeps around the corner.

A truck and two smaller vehicles are parked in front of the warehouse. One is Mr Kalin's car, the other a black Humvee.

Naveed drops to his belly and slides around the corner, edging along behind a low retaining wall, followed closely by Nasera. When he's as close as he dares get, he stops and pulls himself up to look over the top of the wall.

The truck is backed up to the open doors of the warehouse and men are lifting rectangular boxes from it. The boxes are about a metre and a half long and perhaps half a metre in depth and width. They are also clearly quite heavy, for it takes two men to lift each crate down from the truck, and another two to ease them onto the ground before carrying them into the warehouse. Armed guards are stationed around the truck.

Mr Kalin is standing over one box that has been opened, inspecting the contents with another man. Naveed recognises the man by his bulky, overweight frame and thick bushy beard. He is Salar Khan, the local warlord and drug dealer. It was probably his Humvee that almost ran over Anoosheh that day near her school.

'Not bad, Kalin,' the warlord mutters. 'But you're asking too much.'

'They're the latest. You won't find better.'

'Still too much. Remember the cause. It is a noble one.'

Mr Kalin waves his hands about. 'Of course. I'm sure we can come to an arrangement that pleases you.'

'I hope so. And the other? You have plenty of that?'

'Oh yes.' Mr Kalin chuckles. 'Enough to do the job several times over. And it's all safe with me. No one will find it.'

'Very well,' says Salar Khan. 'You'll hear from someone when we're ready.'

He snaps his fingers and a guard rushes to the Humvee, opening the back door. Salar Khan lumbers across to his vehicle.

'Glad to be of service,' Mr Kalin says, scurrying behind.

'Just be ready when the time comes,' the warlord growls as he climbs into the Humvee. His door slams shut and the black vehicle roars off, leaving Mr Kalin in a cloud of diesel smoke. He coughs, waving away the fumes, and turns around.

'Ajala kon! – Hurry up!' he yells at the men. 'I don't have all night, you lazy dogs.'

Naveed strains his neck, trying to catch a glimpse of what's in the open crate. But before he can see anything, one of the workers slaps a lid on top and hammers it down.

He slides out of sight behind the low wall and slithers back to the laneway.

Chapter 21

Naveed arrives at Bagram Airfield early the next morning, Nasera at his side. They wait at the entry control point until Jake comes. He doesn't have Stingray with him this time.

'We're going to focus totally on your dog, mate,' he says, beckoning Naveed through the ECP. 'Did you bring that doll?'

'Yes, Mr Jake.' Naveed points to his bag. 'Is here.'

'Let's get cracking then.'

They go to a quieter area of the base where Jake gets Naveed to spend some time just throwing a ball for Nasera. No matter how often he throws the ball she bounds after it, bringing it back and dropping it at his feet, waiting keenly for him to throw it again.

'See how she loves doing this?' says Jake. 'She can't get enough of it. That's good because we can use it as her reward. Okay so far?'

Naveed shakes his head. 'What reward, Mr Jake?'

'For sniffing out explosives. That's what this is all

about.' Jake holds up a box with the word EXPLOSIVES printed across it in big letters. 'Whenever she smells out one of these nasties, we reward her. We can do it with food but the ball is best. It's in her blood. Understand?'

'I think.' Naveed frowns. 'But how we teach her smell bomb?'

'That's the next step. And that's where the doll comes in.' Jake holds out his hand.

Naveed pulls the ragdoll from his bag and gives it to Jake. Nasera sees this and immediately her ears prick up and her eyes become fixed on the doll.

'Keep a hold of her,' Jake tells Naveed as he walks over to a concrete wall about twenty metres away.

He puts the doll on the wall and places a small lump of what looks like grey putty next to it.

'This is TNT,' he explains. 'It is just one of several explosives we'll train Nasera to recognise. In a moment I'll ask you to let her go. When you do, she'll rush over here and retrieve her toy. She'll do that because she wants to; she likes her toy. But at the same time she will also catch a whiff of the TNT.'

'I see,' says Naveed. 'You make sniffing bomb kind of game, yes?'

'That's right. It's a game, but a deadly serious one. And it takes a lot of training and practice. That's where you come in.'

'Okay. So I let her go now?'

'Not yet. Remember I said she'll rush over to her toy? When she reaches the doll I want you to call out. Tell her to sit and stay and what a good dog she is. Then walk over to her and—'

'And throw ball for reward.'

'Spot on, mate. I said you were a fast learner.' Jake steps well back from the wall. 'Ready to rock and roll, then?'

Naveed frowns. 'Rock and . . .?'

'Don't worry,' Jake replies with a laugh. He points at Nasera. 'Let's see what the girl can do. Let her rip, er, I mean go.'

It happens exactly as Jake said. Naveed is amazed. As soon as he releases Nasera she runs straight to the concrete wall and peers at the ragdoll. But as she is about to reach up and grab it in her mouth he calls out.

'Sug khob – good dog,' he shouts, holding up one hand. 'Sit. Stay right there.' She obeys. He walks over and pats her. 'Sug beseyar khob – *very* good dog.'

Then he produces her ball. She brightens at once, and races off when he throws it across the field, quickly returning to his side and dropping it at his feet.

'Brilliant,' Jake shouts. He strides over and slaps a reassuring hand on Naveed's shoulder. 'Lesson number one passed with flying colours.'

Jake and Naveed spend the rest of the morning repeating this exercise with a number of variations aimed at both challenging Nasera and keeping her interested.

'I want the scent of this explosive firmly imprinted on her brain,' Jake explains. 'But we mustn't let her get bored,' he adds, going on to pair the doll and the TNT in a range of different places.

He puts them under a car and on the back of a quad bike, in a flower pot, in the fork of a tree, on some building rubble, and in the tray of a pickup truck, all the time allowing Nasera to see what he is doing while Naveed holds her back. Then, when she's released, she runs directly to the spot and is promptly rewarded.

'Let's try something a bit different with her now,' Jake says after many of these sessions.

He sits the doll and the explosive next to a garbage bin. Nasera goes straight to the spot, of course – too easy. But the next time, Jake places the items *inside* the bin. That tests her out. She circles the bin several times, whining and sniffing at it. She knows her toy is in there; she's seen Jake place it there. She stands up on her back legs and tries to push the bin over. But it won't budge. In the end she sits on her haunches, turns to Naveed and barks.

'Fantastic,' Jake yells. 'Wonderful. That is *exactly* what I wanted her to do. She's letting you know that she's found the toy. We've still got a long way to go, but believe me, she has just taken a really big step forward. In time that will be her way of telling you that she has found a landmine or some other explosive device.' Jake beckons to Naveed. 'Come on, mate. She deserves a bloody big reward.'

Naveed hugs Nasera and throws the ball for her, while Jake jots down some notes in an exercise book. When he's finished writing he glances at his watch.

'We're going to wrap it up there, Naveed. She's just done over three hours' solid training and she stayed focused the whole time. That's darn good. If she can keep that up, you two are going to be real winners.'

Naveed grins. 'Thank you, Mr Jake. I proud of her,' he says, giving Nasera another hug.

'And so you should be,' Jake adds as they walk back through the base. 'She's a smart dog, an even faster learner than I expected. Which means we are going to have to keep her fully occupied in these training sessions to make sure she doesn't get bored.'

'So we come again tomorrow?'

'You bet. And the next day, and the next, for the rest of the week. Are you okay with that?'

Okay? Of course Naveed is okay. A huge window has been opened in his life, letting in loads of light and fresh air. He can't get enough of it.

'No sweats, Mr Jake,' he says as they reach the entry control point. 'Is very okay.'

After Naveed farewells Jake he strides down the long avenue leading off Bagram Airfield, feeling somehow taller. He can't help noticing something different about Nasera as well. She's walking much closer to him than usual, almost treading in his footsteps. And she's watching him all the time, as if not wanting to let him out of her sight. Naveed can't put his finger on it exactly, but something important has definitely happened to him and Nasera, to each individually as well as between them.

He passes the long line of jingle trucks, pickups and motorbikes edging their way into the base through the maze of Hesco bags, speed bumps and blast blocks. The vehicles are being systematically inspected by teams of soldiers, each team with a dog on a leash.

'Look,' Naveed says. 'One day that will be us.'

They stop and watch a truck being checked. A dog sniffs the vehicle all over: jumping up onto the back, into the cabin, crawling underneath. The vehicle is okayed and allowed to move on. Naveed goes as well and is soon wandering through the busy community that has grown up outside the base.

He breathes in the lunchtime aromas – kebabs cooking, nan being baked, chestnuts roasting on braziers. The smells are mixed with diesel fumes and dust, but are still delicious enough to cause hunger pangs. He buys a freshly baked slab of nan, and then decides on some chestnuts as well. It's extravagant, he knows, but his mother and sister love them, too. Besides, there's something special about today, something to celebrate.

With the nan under one arm and the warm chestnuts cupped in a newspaper cone, Naveed heads off. As he walks he gazes about, enjoying the clatter and clutter of street life. Some way along the road he comes upon a gathering outside a shop. The people are watching a television in the shop window. Naveed can't actually see the screen, but he doesn't need to, for he can hear a voice that he knows very well – Malalai Farzana.

'Freedom? Oh yes, we have so much freedom in this country,' she sneers. 'Women are free to beg in the streets. Children are free to work their childhood away, free to be violated. Girls are free to stay at home instead of going to school, free to be married off to old men. Mothers are free to sell their children rather than watch them starve to death. Taliban are free to punish us for daring to live. Warlords free to trample all over us and steal what's ours. Look around at your country, fellow Afghans. It is a tragedy. Allah weeps for us.'

Naveed does look around. The crowd is mostly male, of course: just two women in burqas. A few men snigger, but most are listening. Some even nod. Naveed is heartened by this, and pops a chestnut into his mouth, savouring its taste and texture.

But then he suddenly stops chewing.

A black Humvee is parked on the other side of the street. The back window is down a little, and Naveed can just make out a large shadowy figure in the vehicle's dark interior. He wants to move away, but feels riveted to the spot, like a hare in headlights. Then the window slowly rises and the Humvee drives on. As it passes by, Naveed catches a glimpse of himself reflected in the black windows.

He swallows uneasily, Malalai's words now magnified in his mind.

'It does not have to be so, this tragedy we live. We can end it, brothers and sisters. But we have to do it together. Freedom is not just *given* to you. It has to be taken, and that is something only we can do as a people, as a nation! Hear me, brothers and sisters: it is time to *take* our freedom!'

Chapter 22

Over the rest of the week Naveed and Nasera go to Bagram Airfield every morning for about three hours. Jake puts them through a training program that grows increasingly intense with each day.

'I know I'm pushing you guys hard,' he says at one point. 'But Nasera is picking things up so quick that I want to keep moving ahead while she's so focused.'

'Is good, Mr Jake. We here to learn.'

And learn they certainly do. In no time at all Nasera is able to find the ragdoll when she hasn't seen where Jake has placed it.

'That means she's sniffing out the explosive now, not the doll. We don't need the toy anymore. She's made the link; the scent is imprinted.' Jake shakes his head. 'And let me tell you, that has to be a record. This dog never ceases to amaze me.'

After that Jake removes the ragdoll completely from the sessions, and hides the TNT on its own in all sorts of places, making the task more and more difficult.

He buries it in holes on the side of the road, placing it deeper each time. But even beneath twenty centimetres of packed dirt Nasera still manages to pick up the scent.

'That's gotta be a record, too,' Jake says. 'The best I've ever come across is a Labrador that located explosives at just over fifteen centimetres. I reckon Nasera has the makings of a vapour dog. She seems to be able to pick up the scent of explosive in the air, like a vapour drifting through. If so, that makes her *really* special.'

He sets up building searches for Nasera, in warehouses, soldiers' compounds and mess halls, under mattresses, on top of wardrobes, inside drawers and desks. He hides the explosive in laundries and toilet blocks and other places with strong competing smells that might mask the scent of the TNT. But Nasera keeps right on target every time.

'I could take her on to other explosives and stuff,' Jake explains towards the end of the week. 'I'm talking gear like PE4, RPGs and other grenades, plastic landmines that can't be located by metal detectors, and so on. But we might leave that for later; I've no doubt she'll do those ones dead easy. Right now I want to see how she works when we up the stress level.'

So in the exercises after that, Jake increases the noise level around Nasera as she searches for the hidden explosives, to see at what point she becomes too distracted to work effectively. He starts with crow scarers, then goes on to loud engines, recordings of street noises, people shouting, distorted music booming from big speakers, screeches of electronic interference. But he never seems to reach the point where she can no longer work. The whopping blast from an ordnance detonation makes her jump, but she's soon back on the job. She is even able to work close to choppers and jet planes as they take off and land.

'A lot of dogs are really freaked by the noise from those monsters,' he tells Naveed. 'But for Nasera it just seems to be business as usual. She's incredible.'

On the last day Jake tests Nasera in a simulated manoeuvre to see how she copes. As part of the operation he kits out Naveed in a flak vest and helmet. Jake's boss comes along, too, as an observer. They hunker down behind a wall with a platoon of soldiers in the midst of a fierce battle, guns and mortars raging all around them.

'They're firing duds,' yells Jake. 'But this is so close to the real thing. And look at her, will ya?' Nasera lies between them licking her paws. 'Cool as a cucumber.'

'You're not wrong,' his boss agrees. 'She's got real battle 'tude, all right.'

Eventually the 'enemy' in the operation is silenced and it's time for the troops to move forward. But the road has to be checked for booby traps.

'That's you,' says Jake. 'You're on.'

'Time for rock and rolls, yes?' Naveed holds up his finger.

'You said it,' Jake replies with a grin.

They climb over the wall. Naveed has Nasera on a leash.

'The guys have planted an IED somewhere on the road ahead,' Jake's boss explains. He nods at the dog. 'Let's see how she gets on.'

Naveed unclips the leash and Nasera goes straight to work. She paces back and forth across the road, moving steadily forward.

'She's good,' says Jake's boss. 'Methodical, focused, intense.'

It isn't long at all before Nasera finds the IED. She stops immediately, her body stiffens and she stares directly at a spot on the road, her tail poking straight out like a pointer dog. Then she turns her head to Naveed and barks.

'Perfect,' Jake whispers.

Naveed is nervous, worried that he'll make a mistake with Jake's boss and all the soldiers watching. But he takes a deep breath, steps forward and calls to Nasera.

'Sug khob – good dog,' he shouts, raising both arms clearly above his head, one hand in stop mode, the other holding up her ball. 'Stay. Sit.'

Nasera obeys, but keeps her eyes trained on the spot where the IED is planted as Naveed walks towards her. When he reaches her he places a small circular marker at her front paws; it has a red arrow pointing towards the suspected IED. That done, he steps back a few paces and slaps his thigh. The moment Nasera hears this she relaxes and goes straight to Naveed's side, gazing up at him expectantly.

He holds out the ball. She barks until he throws it high. Then she leaps up and catches it mid-flight. The soldiers clap and cheer.

'You're right,' Jake's boss admits. 'She's everything you said she is.' He slaps Jake on the back and then he turns to Naveed. 'Most impressive, young fella. We're going to have to find a place for you and your dog.'

Later that day, when the training program is finished and they're alone together, Naveed turns to Jake.

'I have question, Mr Jake. Your boss, what he mean find place for Nasera and me?'

They are passing the very same tree where the training program started over a week ago. They stop and sit together in its shade.

'You two have come a long way in a short time. What you've achieved has confirmed what I knew on day one: that Nasera has the makings of a top search and detection dog, and that you have all it takes to be a top handler.'

'Thank you, Mr Jake.'

'But this is only the start, Naveed. I had to put you and Nasera through this solid week of sessions because I needed to be one hundred and ten per cent certain that you were up to the mark. You see, we are going to recommend that you two be included as a team in a full-time training program that will take months to complete. It's a program operated by Afghans, for Afghans. If you're accepted you'll be paid a wage for the training period, Nasera will be cared for and fed well, and you'll be assured of a job when it's over.'

Naveed gives a gasp of excitement, but Jake holds up his hands.

'Hang on, mate. Don't get your hopes too high just yet. I have no doubt you'll be accepted for the course. But because you're so young there is a chance they might insist you wait a few years. I'll tell them that'd be crazy, and I'm fairly sure they'll listen to me.'

'You are very kind, Mr Jake.'

'There'll be paperwork, of course; I'll handle that. But it all may take a few weeks to push through. Maybe even a month. In the meantime we'll try to keep up some exercises and sessions for you and Nasera here on the base.'

'How I ever repay you?'

'Forget it, Naveed. Just watching you two work together this week, and knowing that you'll be making Afghanistan a safer country, is more than enough payment for me, mate.'

Naveed cannot reply. He is too choked up to say anything.

Chapter 23

On the way home that afternoon Naveed stops at several stalls in the bazaar. He buys a good piece of beef, some long-grain rice, eggplants, onions and capsicums, as well as a pastry.

'We'll have a proper meal tonight,' he tells Nasera. 'One fit for a khan. And don't worry,' he adds, holding up a big bone, 'I haven't forgotten about you. We have so much to celebrate.'

Naveed gets to the school before the classes are finished. As he waits, he decides that he won't tell Anoosheh anything yet. He'll keep the good news for when they get home, over dinner.

'I can't wait to see their faces when I tell them,' he says to Nasera, who is sitting at his side. Naveed chuckles, a smile escaping across his face.

'What are you smiling about, big brother?' Anoosheh says, hobbling towards him.

'I'm just happy, that's all. I had a good day. And I bought some treats for tonight. It's time we had a really good meal, I thought.' Naveed looks around. 'Where's Pari?'

'She didn't come today,' his sister replies.

'She didn't come yesterday, either.'

'So?' Anoosheh shrugs as if her friend's absence is of no importance. But Naveed sees the frown sneak across her brow, and knows better.

'Pari loves school. She wouldn't miss it for anything. Is something wrong?'

'You're always so full of questions, brother,' Anoosheh snaps. 'How should I know?' She moves off before he can ask more.

They walk most of the way home in tense silence, Anoosheh clumping along angrily. As they near the long lane leading to their house Naveed thinks that perhaps he should reveal his good news to brighten her spirits. But before he can do so, she stops and turns to him.

'It's not fair,' she says, bitterness in her voice. 'It's not right.'

'What are you talking about? What's not right?'

'I discovered who is taking Pari as his wife.' She winces and then spits out the name like poison. 'Salar Khan!'

'What?' Naveed steps back as if he's been slapped across the face. 'But he's—'

'Yes, he's old and fat and ugly and cruel, and everything that's horrible. He's a monster driving around in his big black Humvee. And Pari is to be sacrificed to that *creature.*'

'There must be something we can do.'

'Don't be ridiculous, brother. We're nobodies. What could we do? Her family is poor. They'll take what they're given – that's how things work.' Anoosheh sighs. 'Her life will be a misery.'

Anoosheh hurries off. Naveed stares after her, too stunned to move. He feels as if he's going to be ill at any moment. When he does eventually move, his gait is more of a stagger than anything, the wobble of a blind man. And as he walks, the words of Malalai Farzana turn over in his head.

Girls are free to stay at home instead of going to school, free to be married off to old men. Married off to old men! Look around at your country, fellow Afghans. It is a tragedy. Allah weeps for us.

Only when a shadow crosses his path and Nasera growls does Naveed come out of his trance.

'Mr Kalin,' he mutters. 'I didn't see you there.'

'No. You're as bad as your sister.'

Naveed is in the part of the lane that passes Mr Kalin's warehouse. A truck has just finished unloading.

'I'm sorry, sir. I was thinking about things,' Naveed says.

'You need to teach that sister of yours some manners. She nearly knocked me over and she didn't say a thing.'

Naveed almost apologises for Anoosheh. But then a wave of anger washes over him at the arrogance of this man.

'Perhaps you haven't noticed, Mr Kalin, but my little sister has no legs.'

'I'm not blind. Of course I know she's a cripple. I'm talking about manners.'

'So am I.' Naveed keeps his gaze fixed on Mr Kalin.

The landlord narrows his eyes. 'My, you are the proud one, aren't you?' he sneers.

'When it comes to family, we should all be proud. Don't you agree, sir?'

Mr Kalin laughs. 'I'm glad to hear that. *Very* glad.'

Naveed frowns at Mr Kalin's tone.

'Don't worry, boy. I have a surprise for you, that's all. And he happens to be *family*.'

Mr Kalin snaps his fingers and a youth several years older than Naveed appears from behind the warehouse door. He is gaunt, his skin sallow, his features skeletal. He is smiling but there is no happiness in his face, and it takes Naveed a moment to actually recognise him.

'Cousin Akmed,' he stammers, trying not to sound shocked.

The youth nods and steps forward, a tattered bag slung over his shoulder. They hug, Naveed immediately struck by how feeble his cousin's embrace is and how bony his body.

'It's been such a long time.'

'Yes,' Akmed replies in a wispy, faraway voice, but has nothing else to add.

'A long time, indeed,' Mr Kalin says. 'More than two years, I believe. Your cousin has been in Pakistan, at one of the very best madrasas. He's been improving himself. Spiritually. Isn't that so, Akmed?'

'Yes,' the youth says again, although he doesn't sound

124

all that sure. He seems to flinch when Mr Kalin speaks to him. He is also watching Nasera closely, perhaps nervous of her as well. Naveed is about to assure him that he need not fear the dog. But Mr Kalin speaks first.

'Akmed is just passing through and is in need of somewhere to stay,' he continues. 'When I heard, I immediately thought of you, Naveed. I knew you'd love to take him in, being so proud of *family*.'

'I would,' Naveed replies, smiling apologetically at his cousin. 'But ours is such a tiny home. You may—'

'Only for a few days,' Akmed explains. 'And I won't get in anyone's way, I promise. A few days and I won't ever bother you again.'

'Forgive me, I didn't mean that. You are more than welcome to stay in our house. I only meant that you may be cramped and uncomfortable.'

'Mohem nist – no problem, cousin. Allah gives me all the comfort I need, wherever I am.'

'That's settled, then,' says Mr Kalin, slapping his arms around the boys' shoulders. 'I can't tell you how good it makes me feel bringing you together like this.' He pushes them on their way. 'Off you go. And make the most of each other's company while you can.'

Naveed grits his teeth as he walks down the lane, seething at Mr Kalin's hypocrisy, despising his false friendliness.

'Khuk! Korreh khar! Pig! Son of a donkey!' he mutters and then peeps at his cousin.

But Akmed seems not to have heard. He stares ahead, as if in a daze.

When they reach the alcove into his home, Naveed glances back along the lane. Mr Kalin is still watching them. Nasera is looking back as well. She growls.

Chapter 24

It is a difficult evening for Naveed and his family. Akmed is a dark cloud that has invaded their home, and nothing they do seems to lighten him.

Naveed's mother rushes to embrace her nephew the moment she sees him, her face bright with joy. Anoosheh even pushes aside her dejection about Pari and tries to be her playful self. They serve him chai and kishmish, and shower him with questions. But Akmed is awkward and self-conscious through it all, answering their questions with a yes or no before lapsing into silence again. At times he even seems to be brooding, as if trapped in his own thoughts.

At one point, just before the evening meal is served, Anoosheh makes a desperate effort to lift Akmed's mood by giving a short hip-hop demonstration. Naveed knows it's a mistake and tries to catch her eye to warn her. But to no avail. She goes ahead with her performance. Naveed loves the act, and laughs. Their mother laughs as well. But Akmed doesn't. He stares at Anoosheh as she spins and twists about the room on her stumps, supported by crutches, his brow knitted, his lips pursed, one hand pressing on his copy of the Quran.

'There,' Anoosheh says when she has finished. 'That's hip hop. I can give you a lesson if you wish, cousin Akmed?'

She reaches out to him, smiling. But Akmed pulls back.

'What's the matter?' A nervous laugh escapes from her lips. 'Don't you care for dancing?'

Akmed's reply is quiet, but the tremor in his voice is like anger on a leash.

'I can only tell you the Prophet's words, Allah bless him and give him peace. Mohammed said: *Allah has sent me to eradicate musicals, pipes and the habits of jahiliyyah, the old ways that existed before Islam.* I'm sorry, little cousin, but that sort of dancing is jahiliyyah. It is haram, forbidden.'

Anoosheh's smile fades. Naveed sees this and speaks up at once.

'Come now, cousin. Anoosheh is only playing, having fun. There's no harm in that. How can it be forbidden?'

'Of course, you're right,' Akmed replies, pursing his lips. 'Children must be allowed to play. But she will not always be a child. She is not that far from the age of puberty, I suspect, and that sort of *excessive* dancing would not be fitting for a Muslim girl who wants to live in a righteous way. That is all I am saying.'

Anoosheh's face drops and a tense silence invades the little room. Naveed doesn't know what to say. Cousin

Akmed was harsh and strict in his words to Anoosheh, but Naveed is nervous of replying in case he frees his own anger. Luckily his mother saves the day, announcing it is time to eat.

The meal helps to break the tension that has built up. Naveed casts his eyes over the feast his mother has prepared. She's made a plate of ashak, leek dumplings coated with her own special quroot, mint and garlic sauce. There's a large chapli kebab, a round flat patty of minced meat and flour served with nan. He notices his very favourite dish as well, qabili palao, baked rice with fried raisins, finely sliced carrots and nuts. And there are side dishes, too: several torshi – pickles – and fruits and spiced vegetables – along with chutney and yoghurt.

'Wonderful, Madar,' he says, proud of what she's created at such short notice to honour Akmed.

Anoosheh agrees with an enthusiastic nod. So does Akmed, and the dinner passes quietly with a mix of smiles and pleasantries.

When finished, their cousin sits back, satiated, wiping scraps of food from his wispy beard.

'Thanks be to Allah for feeding us so well,' he says. Taking the copy of the Quran that has been by his side the whole evening, Akmed raises it to his lips and lightly kisses it. 'How fortunate we are.'

Naveed flinches. It was a good meal, yes, but he can't help feeling that Allah was not the only one involved in creating it. After all, he was the one who bought the food, and his mother and sister were the ones who prepared the meal. They'd even found extra rice to make sure

Akmed got his fill – which he did, wolfing down the food as if he were starving.

So a word of appreciation would be nice, Naveed thinks. But he bites his tongue. He knows only too well that Akmed has reasons for being the way he is – dark reasons that cut to his very soul, reasons that made him run away to Pakistan and bury himself in a madrasa for all that time.

Anoosheh stirs and huffs. Naveed can see that she is still upset. And perhaps Akmed feels the tension as well, for in the very next moment he speaks again.

'What am I saying? How rude of me. Bebakhshid – sorry. It is *you* three I should be thanking. I'd forgotten how good food can taste. Ah, such memories.'

Naveed hears the sadness in his cousin's voice. He glances at him and is surprised to see that Akmed is staring straight back. As far as he can recall, his cousin has not once looked directly at any of them for more than a moment. Even when laying down the law about hip hopping, he didn't look Anoosheh in the eye, or anyone else for that matter. But now he is definitely peering into Naveed's eyes, searching them as he continues talking.

'You have been most kind and made me feel very welcome. I know I am a burden and that you do not really want me here, but—'

'No, Akmed,' Naveed interrupts. 'We—'

'Please allow me to finish, cousin. I have wanted to say this all evening, and cannot rest until I have.' Akmed puts down the Quran. 'I want you to understand that you need not worry. I will not trouble you for long. As I said, I ask for only a few days. Then I will be gone, I promise.'

For the first time Naveed actually senses a real person in his cousin. It's as if there's someone trapped behind the eyes staring back at him. But he doesn't know how to reply. It is his mother who speaks.

'You must not say such things, nephew, let alone think them. You will always be welcome under our roof, however humble it might be. You will always be welcome to eat with us, however meagre our food. You will always be in our thoughts and hearts, for you are the son of my husband's brother. You are family, Akmed.'

Naveed feels proud of his mother, and ashamed of his own negative thoughts towards his cousin.

'Thank you, aunty,' Akmed replies. 'Your kindness is great, may Allah bless you. May Allah bless all of you. I am not worthy of such kindness.' He stands, the Quran in his hand again. 'And now, if you do not mind, I will take a walk in the night.'

'Do you wish me to come as well?' asks Naveed, getting to his feet.

'Please, no.' Akmed shakes his head. 'It is not necessary, cousin. And I will not be good company, anyway, for I wish to speak with God.' He makes his way awkwardly towards the door. 'Do not wait up for me. I will be some time.' He bows his head and leaves the room.

Chapter 25

As soon as Akmed has gone Anoosheh utters a long sigh and pretends to tear out her hair.

'Ayee! He's awful. Please make him not return. I don't think I can take another second of him.'

'That's enough, daughter,' her mother whispers, pressing a finger to her lips.

'Don't worry, Madar, he won't hear me. He'll be too busy talking to God.'

'Stop it, Anoosheh, this moment!'

'Why? Why should we have to put up with—'

'There are many reasons. Because he is family. Because he was not always like this. And because he has suffered. Believe me, daughter, Akmed has suffered.'

Anoosheh lets out a bitter laugh. 'What? And I haven't, Madar?'

'Of course you have, my darling. But your suffering is not an excuse to ignore the suffering of others. Indeed, it should make you more sympathetic to their plight.'

Anoosheh's mother sits down next to her daughter.

'You didn't know the other Akmed. Naveed did, though only briefly. He was a wonderful boy, so full of life and fun. That Akmed would have hip hopped with you all night. He only had to open his mouth and he made us all laugh. Your father loved him greatly.'

'Impossible, Madar. He—'

'Shush, child. It was the accident that changed him. That's what the Americans called it – *an unfortunate accident*. His sister's wedding was mistakenly targeted as a Taliban gathering by one of their drones. Akmed's three sisters, one brother and both parents were all killed – his entire family. There was nothing left. Only Akmed survived, barely. There was a big gash across his neck where a piece of shrapnel almost decapitated him. It is just a scar now, but a much bigger wound inside hasn't even begun to heal. Perhaps it never will.'

Anoosheh's mother stands.

'That was the day the happy Akmed died. If only you'd known him, little Noosh. If only.'

The three of them clean up in silence, washing and drying the dishes in the outside alcove. Nasera sits in the lane, watching them, aware of the change in the family.

Later, as they lie on their toshaks, Anoosheh breaks the silence.

'You know the saddest thing about our country?' Her question hangs in the dark for a while. 'There is nothing special about Akmed's story. It is everywhere.'

Naveed falls asleep clutching his own good news deep in his heart, a little beacon of hope.

Don't worry, Padar, I'll tell them soon enough. When the time is right.

❖❖❖

Naveed sits up, shaken from his deep sleep by a noise. A scream, he thinks, and listens intently in the dark. Almost immediately it's there again, a shriek of fear. Outside.

'Komak!'

It's his cousin yelling for help. Naveed scrambles to his feet, rushes across the room and out into the night. Akmed is on the ground in the lane, cringing against a wall, blubbering like a terrified child.

'Leave me alone!' The ghostly shape of Nasera stands beside him. 'Gom shoo – go away!'

Nasera is not harming Akmed in any way. She's not even growling. In fact as far as Naveed can see all she's doing is sniffing him. He calls her off at once.

'Come,' he snaps, slapping the side of his leg. 'Here to me.'

Nasera immediately pulls back and joins Naveed.

Akmed stands. 'I thought she would tear me to pieces.'

'I'm sorry, cousin, but she was only protecting us. And she wouldn't have harmed you unless you tried to harm us.' Naveed steps towards Akmed. 'Please, don't be frightened. She won't hurt you, not with me here.'

Akmed relaxes a little but still watches the dog warily. Nasera is stretching her neck towards him, her nose testing the air.

'Why is she doing that?'

Naveed laughs. 'She likes you, that's all. And a lot, by the look of it.' He pats the dog and pulls her away. 'Enough, girl. Go to bed.'

Nasera eyes Akmed for a moment, then does as she's told, curling up next to her ragdoll.

'Come, cousin,' Naveed adds. 'You need to sleep as well. You must be exhausted.'

'I am indeed,' Akmed says with a yawn. 'More than you can know.'

They enter the house and bid each other goodnight. But although it is late and Akmed claims to be exhausted, he doesn't fall asleep immediately, Naveed can tell by his breathing. And he can see his cousin's outline in the dark, lying on his back, staring up at the ceiling, hands crossed over his chest.

It is almost an hour before Naveed's cousin sighs, rolls onto his side and falls asleep.

When Naveed wakes in the morning, Akmed has already gone. There is no sign of him, his toshak gone. It's as if yesterday and last night never happened.

'Do you think he's gone for good?' Anoosheh asks over breakfast.

'I hope not,' her mother replies. 'He's such a troubled soul. I hope we can help him.'

Naveed says nothing. He can't decide how he feels about his cousin. One part of Akmed upsets Naveed, even angers him. Another part makes him feel great pity. And the shadow he has left in the house prevents

Naveed from revealing the good news he has. He longs to tell his mother and Anoosheh all about what he's been doing at Bagram with Nasera, what an amazing dog she is, and how he could have a proper job from it all, one that he would feel really proud of.

Perhaps this afternoon, or this evening, he tells himself as he finishes breakfast and stands.

'Come on, little sister,' he says. 'Time for school.'

Chapter 26

The traffic is much busier than usual on the road that leads past Anoosheh's school. The vehicles seem more edgy and aggressive. Naveed makes his sister stay with him as they negotiate their way on the narrow side-strip meant for pedestrians but often used by impatient drivers. And there are plenty of those today. More than once they have to flatten themselves against a building or fence as a vehicle roars past, horn blaring, dust and gravel whipped up behind it.

'I've never seen it so busy,' Naveed says. 'There must be something big on in town today.'

When they reach the school, people are standing about talking excitedly. The principal, Mr Farzin, is near the front gate speaking to a large group.

'There is a big demonstration at Bagram Airfield,' he explains.

'What about?' someone asks.

'I cannot say for sure. All I know is that people are angry, and the Americans are very nervous. My advice to all of you is to stay away. The situation could become dangerous.'

Naveed doesn't take the principal's advice. He decides to find out for himself what's going on, and so makes his way into town. Before he is even close to Bagram Airfield he can hear the chanting and yelling. Cries of 'Allahu Akbar – God is greater' echo across town, mixed with shouts of 'Die, foreigners, die!' and 'Burn the blasphemers!'

When he eventually reaches the base Naveed is shocked by the size of the crowd, and glad that he has left Nasera at home. There are thousands of people, mainly men – especially young ones – but boys as well, many younger than Naveed. People line the streets and roads. They stand on the rickety roofs of shacks and shanties, cram onto verandas and staircases, shaking their fists and howling abuse at the soldiers. Others press against rolls of razor wire and the mesh fences around the base, screaming their anger and hatred.

A black pall of acrid smoke rises from a pile of flaming tyres onto which the protestors throw anything that will burn. They hurl rocks and petrol bombs at the base; they fire slingshots, catapults and antiquated hunting rifles. They strike at the security fence with farming implements, lumps of wood, lengths of metal pipe, anything they can find.

Guards in the watchtowers respond with rubber bullets, but this does nothing to quell the rising tide of violence; it only infuriates the demonstrators even more.

Groups hide behind concrete blast blocks and Hesco bags to fire their makeshift weapons; they squat behind market stalls, overturned tables and vehicles.

A life-size scarecrow figure is held high on a wooden pole, arms and legs flopping about, an American flag hanging from its neck. The crowd cheers as the figure is plunged into the bonfire and catches alight. As it burns it is paraded through the street to even louder cheers before being thrown to the ground and stamped upon in a frenzy.

A young man leaps onto the back of a truck; Naveed guesses he's Taliban, but can't be sure. An older man whose hands and arms are bandaged to the elbow is helped up as well. He weeps, pressing his bandaged hands to his face. The younger man comforts him and then steps forward cradling a copy of the Quran that has been partially burned, its cover and many of its pages blackened and charred. His face taut with fury, he raises the book to his lips and kisses it. Then he turns to the crowd.

'They have done it again, these foreign serpents that have slithered into our land and poisoned us with their evil ways.' He holds the book high. 'See! They have defiled the sacred word of Allah yet again.'

'Allahu Akbar!' the crowd roars in reply. Naveed glances about and sees anger and hate on the faces all around him.

'Two years ago they were caught burning God's word. Now we have caught them again. For all we know they have been doing it all the time in there, behind those

139

walls. Truly their evil knows no bounds. We must visit Allah's wrath upon them.'

'Allahu Akbar!' The crowd roars again, louder, their voices pushing in on Naveed. He moves closer to the truck, his eyes fixed on the young man.

'This is only one of many holy books they have desecrated. Last night, under the cover of darkness, like the cowards they are, they threw untold numbers of the sacred book into a pit and turned their foul fires upon them.'

'Death to the foreign devils,' the crowd chants until the young man holds up his hands.

'And they would have got away with their evil crime had it not been for our brother here.' He draws the older man forward and has him raise his arms in the air. 'This brave man leaped into that pit of fire to save Allah's holy words. See how he weeps? That is because there were many books he could not pull from the flames. His hands would have been burned away. Do not torture yourself, brother. Allah knows you did your best, and blesses you.'

He embraces the older man and then presents him to the cheering crowd. A group lifts the bandaged man from the back of the truck and carries him off on their shoulders, singing his praises and cursing the foreigners. Their curses swarm around Naveed, forcing their way into his head. Into his heart.

'But that is *still* not all these dogs have done to despoil our holiest of books,' the young man goes on, his voice louder than ever. 'Oh no. They have torn out pages. They have ripped them to pieces. They have trampled them into the dirt. And then—' The young man stops. He closes his eyes and his face trembles. 'It so sickens me to think on this that I cannot even utter the exact words. But believe me when I tell you – they have committed the foulest of acts upon Allah's words.' He takes a deep breath and screams: 'The *foulest* of acts!'

The crowd around the truck bursts into a frenzy of abuse. Some rush to the perimeter fence and join those pounding upon it. Others grab anything they can lay their hands on – stones, bricks, wood, *anything* – and hurl it at the military base in blind frustration and fury. Others still march off to spread the young man's revelations.

Naveed is stunned, sickened by what he's heard. He wanders off, staring at the ground, body shaking, insides churning, mind a whirlpool. His tears make everything a blur – the base, the protestors, his whole world.

All that unspeakable evil was probably going on while he was in there with Nasera throughout the week. And Mr Jake would have known. *He must have known*, that's where he lives. And yet he said nothing. Naveed suddenly feels dirty, disgusted that he could ever have had anything to do with the military base.

'Pit of filth!' That's what the young man on the back of the truck said. *'Den of infidels!'* That's what everyone yelled. What was he thinking, going in there and letting them fill his head with ideas? *Blasphemers!* He's been cheated, that's what's happened. The hope that Mr Jake held out to him was nothing but a lie, a trick to lure him in and make him one of them.

Tricked! Mr Jake was only pretending to be his friend. All along he was just part of the huge military monster ravaging their country in the name of freedom and democracy. Part of the great big lie.

Naveed lifts his gaze and looks about. His tears have cleared a little and he sees that he's near the front of a crowd in the narrow approach to Entry Control Point One. A temporary wall of Hesco bags and razor wire holds them back as they shout abuse and threats. About a hundred metres ahead is a heavily armed force of American soldiers, backed by a squad of turtleback Humvees, their weapons trained on the protestors.

Naveed stares at the soldiers, anger and confusion stewing in him, stirred by the chanting all around. He opens his mouth to scream out loud like everyone else. But then he sees Mr Jake, and chokes on his own pain and fury.

Chapter 27

'I just want to know exactly what happened last night.'
Jake is standing with Private Horten at Entry Control
Point One.

Horten shrugs. 'A few books got torched, that's all.'

'A few *holy* books, you mean. Qurans.'

'Quran, Shmuran. What is it with these freakin' hajis?
It's just a book, for Christ's sake!'

'No, Horten. It's much more than a book to Muslims.
The Quran is a sacred object. It's Allah's word direct,
you know, straight from the big dude's mouth.'

'Huh! I betcha half of them can't even read.'

'That's beside the point. They know that burning
the Quran is an outright insult to their God. It's
about the worst thing you can do. That's why they're
so upset, mate. If a big part of this war is winning
hearts and minds, we've just shot ourselves in the foot
real bad.'

'Okay, I grant you there are some people out there
who are genuinely upset, and my heart bleeds for them.

Boo hoo. But I also reckon there's a damn sight more who just want an excuse to fight us. And we ain't never gonna win their hearts and minds.'

'Sure, but burning their holy book is just playing into the extremists' hands, and they know how to whip the others up. Take a look. They've got the crowd pumped, mate.'

'You're not wrong.' Horten nods, giving Jake a friendly thump. 'But you know what? I couldn't give a damn, 'cause in a couple of days I'm out of this hole. And I ain't coming back.' He whoops with delight. 'Oooooeeee! Utah, here I come.' He grabs Jake in a bear hug. 'I'm going home, Aussie. Eat your heart out.'

Jake laughs as Horten wrestles with him, but eventually breaks free and turns towards the mob of protestors.

He sees a wall of shaking fists, a wall of faces contorted with fury, hurling abuse. Mostly young men, but there are kids as well; so many, he thinks, as he scans the scene. Too young to have such hate in their hearts.

Suddenly one face catches his eye. He stops and stares hard.

'Bloody hell!'

'What's the matter?' Horten asks, readying his M16.

'It's Naveed.'

'You mean that kid you've been helping out, the one with the dog? The one that sold me the D-30 shell?'

Jake nods. 'Look at him,' he says, pointing.

Horten searches the faces until he spots Naveed. 'Whoa. That is one upset kid. He's sure giving you the big dirty. There's a lotta anger in that face, man.'

There's more than anger, Jake thinks as he stares back. Naveed isn't yelling or gesturing. He's simply staring. But what a stare it is. Jake cannot take his eyes off the boy. Naveed stands totally still among a swirling mass of movement and sound, glaring at Jake with a look that sends a shudder right through him. It's all there – confusion, disillusionment, anger, betrayal and hurt. More than anything, hurt.

Horten slaps his arm around Jake's shoulders. 'Don't take it too hard, pal. That's hajis for you. You've worked your butt off for that kid, and look at the payback. Gratitude, ha. They don't know the meaning of the word.'

'I've got to talk to him,' Jake says, pushing away from Horten.

'Whoa! I wouldn't go out there if I was you.'

'I have to explain. He's just a boy. He doesn't understand.'

'They'll tear you to pieces.'

Jake leaps over the blast panel. Horten yells at him to come back, but then follows a few seconds later.

Jake strides towards the protestors, but he's too late. Naveed has already gone.

'Naveed!' he shouts, desperately searching for the boy. But he's nowhere to be seen, swallowed by the crowd.

Jake stops. He's about halfway between the entry control point and the protestors. He stares at the angry mob, every face a reminder of Naveed's. With a mix of regret, frustration and failure, along with a deep sense of sadness, Jake turns and begins to walk back towards

Horten. But before he's gone far, the American is yelling and pointing behind him.

'Get the hell outta there!'

Jake spins around in time to see the dark figure at the edge of the crowd aiming an RPG launcher straight at him. He instantly drops to the ground and the rocket-propelled grenade howls overhead.

Horten isn't so lucky.

Naveed hears Jake call as he runs through the crowd, but keeps going. He wants to get as far away as possible from all of this, to leave the whole horrible nightmare behind.

Naveed!

He thinks he hears his name again, but stumbles on, everything a blur once more, sounds and voices swirling. He bumps into people, trips and falls, scrambles to his feet and staggers on.

He hears an explosion behind, or thinks he does. He hears the crowd cheer – *Allahu Akbar*. And then the gunfire, rapid bursts, followed by screams.

He clamps his hands over his ears and keeps running.

Chapter 28

The rioting continues for another three days. Naveed tries to stay away, but several times finds himself lured back, moth-like, to the flaring violence. He stands well away on such occasions, observing from a distance, yet still gripped by this creature of war.

Demonstrators pour in from other parts of Afghanistan – Herat, Jalalabad, Kabul, Helmand. Naveed watches them swarm around the airfield like flies on a carcass, feeding their frenzy of hate. More effigies are torched and trampled, more flags burned, more bonfires of tyres belch black smoke into the sky.

Attacks on the base grow more daring. Attempts to scale the perimeter fence are carried out in different locations. A suicide bomber even makes it as far as one of the entry control points on day two, killing three marines and badly injuring several others. Naveed only hears rumours of this, for he refuses to go anywhere near the entry control points lest he see Mr Jake again.

Night attacks increase, too, despite total floodlighting and round-the-clock surveillance. And loudspeakers blare out constantly, inciting all true Muslims to avenge the insults upon God. Naveed hears them as he lies in bed and feels their pull.

On the third night, unable to resist, he creeps back to the base and watches from a ditch as a major attack is made. About twenty protestors break through the first perimeter fence at the northern end of Bagram Airfield, backed by sustained mortar fire. A fierce fight rages for hours, turning night into day, ending only when all the attackers are killed.

After that defeat the enthusiasm of the demonstrators fades. Naveed doesn't go near the base again. There are vehement speeches the next day, trying to whip up anger, but they fail. By the afternoon, everyone has drifted away.

The riots are over, and Bagram Airfield heaves a huge sigh of relief.

That same afternoon Private James Edward Horten is flown home. He didn't regain consciousness after being hit by the RPG, and died on the last night of the riots. Jake sat at his bedside every chance he got, and talked to him. At one point he thought there was a flicker of recognition, but that was as good as it got for the boy from Utah.

Jake stands at the edge of the airstrip, watching the big C-17 Globemaster carry Horten into the clouds, along with three other casualties of the last few days, and a shipment of Humvees that won't be needed anymore. Stingray sits beside him, and seems to sense his sadness, nudging him with his muzzle.

'Horto got his wish.' Jake glances down at the dog. 'He's going home,' he mutters thickly. 'And he won't be coming back.'

✦✦✦

'O my Lord, forgive me.'

Naveed is out in the countryside as the big plane climbs across the sky. He's beside an old irrigation ditch, finishing his midday prayer, the Namaaz e Zohr.

'O my Lord, forgive me,' he whispers again, drawing the last of the four raka'at to a close.

Nasera lies nearby, her huge uncomprehending eyes watching Naveed. He's been different for days now, and she doesn't understand what's wrong. He's been moping around, hardly saying anything, often snapping angrily when he does speak. He hasn't patted her at all, and last night he just tossed her some food as if she didn't matter. At least he's taken her with him today on his walk, the first time in a couple of days.

The roar of the plane slowly fades. Naveed watches its white trail slice the blue sky. He's been walking all day, making himself keep as far away as possible from Bagram Airfield. Not that the base has kept away from him. It's in his head, thoughts that won't go away, questions nagging at the back of his mind.

What do I do, Padar? How do I make sense of all this?

Akmed would know what to do. He would have answers. But then Naveed is not sure he wants those answers.

He saw very little of his cousin during the rioting. Akmed didn't even appear on the first night. Naveed's mother had a meal prepared, but he didn't show up at all. He came home the next night, but was tired and worn out and kept falling asleep during the meal. The next morning he sneaked away while everyone was asleep, and hasn't appeared since.

Naveed is pleased not to have had Akmed around. He has more than enough weighing him down without adding his cousin's gloominess to the burden as well.

He stands and, without a word to Nasera, walks off. She watches, waiting for him to look back over his shoulder or call. But he does neither. When he's almost out of sight she gets up and follows him.

Naveed walks aimlessly, kicking stones out of the way, wishing he could kick his thoughts away as well.

So many people yelling, Padar. I don't know what to think.

Do not be fooled by the loud voices, my son. Empty vessels can make the greatest noise.

That's easy to say, Padar. But sometimes they're the only ones you can hear.

Then you must listen harder. Listen for the quieter voice, the one deep inside. Listen to your heart.

Naveed sighs. Barely aware of anything around him or where he's heading, he eventually ends up at a truck stop on the outskirts of town. About twenty vehicles are parked in the big vacant lot, many of them jingle trucks. A group of drivers squat together, talking, smoking, sipping chai. Others are washing their trucks; a few are polishing them. Naveed gives the scene a sideways glance and hurries on. But then he hears his name being called.

Chapter 29

'Just the person I need.' Mr Omaid is standing at the front of his jingle truck, beckoning. 'Come and earn some money to buy your mother a treat. She deserves one.'

Naveed forces his lips into a smile and walks over to Mr Omaid, who has just finished working on the truck's engine.

'The old girl is giving me trouble,' the truck driver explains as he closes the bonnet. 'She's spluttering all the time. Perhaps a good polish will make her go better. Praise be to Allah for sending you along to help me.' He tosses a rag to Naveed. 'The other side needs a thorough buffing, my boy.'

At first Naveed tackles the job half-heartedly, but after a while finds that it is just what he needs, something to take his mind off the endless brooding. Mr Omaid whistles a tune as he works, occasionally humming and even singing parts of the song. Before long Naveed is humming the tune as well. Soon he is completely lost in his work, briskly rubbing the cloudy waxed duco, section by section, watching his reflection appear in the polished paint.

'Perfect.'

Naveed is startled from his reverie by Mr Omaid. The truck driver stands behind him, hands on hips, nodding in approval.

'That's the best job I've ever seen,' he says, flipping Naveed a coin. 'Excellent work.'

Naveed steps back to inspect the truck, and can't help feeling a tingle of satisfaction. The vehicle looks fantastic. The painted parts shining bright and happy make him want to smile, while the glow of chrome in the setting sun sparks a little warmth inside him that wasn't there before.

Mr Omaid pats him on the back. 'How time flies when you're enjoying yourself, eh? Come along then,' he says. 'I'll drive you home.'

Naveed clambers onto the running board and hops into the cabin in a flash. He loves going in the truck; it sits up so high above everyone and makes such a great noise. Mr Omaid joins him, but doesn't start the engine at once. Instead he turns to Naveed.

'Tell me, young man. How is your mother?'

'She is as well as can be expected, Mr Omaid, thanks be to God.'

'It was good to see her, to see all of you, I mean, at the kite-flying competition. I enjoyed myself very much. Perhaps we could do it again before too long. Why, we could even drive into the countryside to picnic, for instance. In my truck, that is, if you see what I mean.'

Mr Omaid seems unusually awkward and self-conscious all of a sudden, and Naveed wonders why that is so, even as he hastens to put him at ease.

'It would be most kind of you, Mr Omaid,' he replies. 'I think my mother and sister would love such a treat.'

'Excellent.' The man beams with delight. 'And how is little Noosh? Still racing around everywhere?'

'Oh, yes. She's unstoppable. I think that if she ever grew legs we would never catch her.'

Mr Omaid laughs. 'Ah, how wonderful that would be.' Then he looks directly at Naveed. 'And you?'

'Me?'

Naveed is caught out. He can't tell the truth: that he feels terrible – angry, sad, lost, bewildered. And yet Mr Omaid's intense gaze seems to ask for that. Now Naveed is the one feeling self-conscious. He doesn't know how to reply.

'You're not happy, are you?' Mr Omaid speaks for him. 'I can see it as plain as the nose on your face. You have worries on your mind. There is anger in your heart. And more, I suspect. Am I correct in this?'

Naveed nods. 'You are,' he says. 'You are most correct.'

In the next breath he lets everything spill out, an avalanche of emotion, all the feeling he's held inside since that first day of the riots, when he saw the charred Quran in the hands of that angry young man on the back of the truck. His anger with the Americans for insulting Allah. His hunger for revenge. The shame he feels, for letting himself be drawn into the foreigners' web of deceit.

And the pain, the deep pain from being hurt inside. He spits it all out like bile that has been eating away at him for days.

Mr Omaid listens without interrupting. Even when Naveed finishes he doesn't reply at once.

'You are a good boy,' he says eventually. 'Your heart is pure, and I am sure Allah sees it is so. But you are wrong in this, and I believe your father would tell you as much if he were here.'

'But the Americans, they insulted—'

'Yes, I know, they insulted God, and I condemn them for that. But do you really think Allah needs us to avenge him? Of course not – Allah is everything, we are nothing. And to respond with violence is indeed a much bigger crime. The riots of the last few days, especially the suicide bombers, were wrong, the work of radicals who only want to fan the flames of hate within us. Believe me, they are not defending the faith. They are exploiting our religious feelings for their own evil ends. They don't want us to heal our wounded country. They want to open those wounds further and bleed us to death. These acts of violence harm the people of Afghanistan much more than they help us.'

Naveed is surprised at how passionate the normally mild-mannered Mr Omaid has suddenly become.

'I know there are bad people among the foreigners here in our land. But there are many more good people who want to help us get back on our feet again. Your friend, Mr Jake, is one of those. I know of his work with you and your dog. He is helping you to do something that will make our country a safer place in which to live. He is a good man whose heart is in the right place. Do not judge him harshly. Do not spurn his offers of help.'

Mr Omaid pauses, fumbling with the keys of the truck. A piece of the sun glows on the horizon like a tiny but fierce ball of fire. Naveed watches it burn, the glow warming him inside as words echo in his thoughts.

'Anyway, I've kept you long enough,' Mr Omaid says after a while. 'We really should be going. But haven't you forgotten someone?'

'Of course,' Naveed gasps. He looks out the window. Nasera is sitting on the ground staring up at him, waiting patiently. 'Is she allowed in with us?'

'Most definitely. She is a very special dog, with very special skills. One day soon you and she will save many, many Afghan lives. I'd be honoured to have her sit in my truck.'

Naveed calls Nasera. She leaps aboard and is soon sitting up between the two of them.

Mr Omaid turns the key in the ignition, but the truck only splutters. He curses under his breath.

'I have work at Bagram Airfield tomorrow. I need the old girl to behave.' He raises his hands and eyes to heaven in supplication. 'Please be kind to me, Allah,' he cries, turning the key in the ignition once more.

The truck grumbles and rumbles for a while, back-fires twice, and then suddenly roars to life.

Chapter 30

Jake is on the steps outside his B-hut, just after lunch. He can't get Naveed out of his mind. He can still see the boy's face among the rioters, full of confusion and anger. And yet there had been such hope and promise. Naveed and Nasera were total winners, able to do untold good in a country where good didn't happen nearly enough.

There is something else bothering Jake, too. He has just received confirmation from the hospital that they will assess Anoosheh for prosthetic legs. But for that to happen the family will have to bring her to Bagram Airfield.

Jake clenches his fists and curses with frustration. If only he could just talk to Naveed. But he knows that's not likely to happen. The boy won't be coming back; his face at the riots made that clear. And as for finding him, Jake wouldn't have a clue where to start.

'Let it go,' Jake's boss told him only that morning. 'You win some, you lose some; that's life. He's just a kid anyway.'

157

'No,' Jake mutters to himself. Some things are far too important to just let go of.

He gazes across at several jingle trucks that have stopped on the other side of the road. One has broken down; its bonnet up, drivers gathered around, poking at the engine. Jake watches them for a moment and suddenly recognises one of the drivers. He dashes over the road.

'Excuse me,' he says to the man. 'Remember me? We met at the park with the kites. Remember?'

Of course Mr Omaid recognises Jake, but he knows almost no English. He smiles and nods, struggling to reply. 'Yes, friend, er, Naveed,' he says.

'That's right. I need to talk to Naveed. Understand?'

Mr Omaid smiles nervously and keeps nodding. 'Naveed friend, yes.'

'Yeah, that's it. But—' Jake turns to the other drivers. 'Any of you speak English?'

'I do,' one replies.

Jake sighs with relief. 'Ripper, mate.'

'Hundreds of our people have been injured. More than fifty have died. That's over fifty martyrs. Allah will embrace them and give them a special place in Paradise.'

Naveed wishes Akmed would stop this talk. He glances at Anoosheh – the cousins are walking her home from school – and shrugs. He's been politely listening to Akmed ever since leaving home to pick up his sister.

He had been looking forward to a quiet stroll by himself, but Akmed insisted on joining him. No sooner had they left home than he began talking – ranting, really – about foreign devils and such matters, and he hasn't drawn breath since. Naveed is not sure how much more he can take before saying something. Anoosheh looks as if she'll explode at any moment.

The riots at Bagram Airfield seem to have sparked a change in his cousin, Naveed can't help thinking. The young man who arrived at their house less than a week ago was moody and brooding; he kept to himself and had almost nothing to say. The Akmed who turned up again that morning and is now walking at Naveed's side, Quran in hand, is outspoken and strident in his views. And now his rant builds to a climax.

'They have special kill teams, undercover squads that murder Afghans. There are snipers who pick off people in the street just for fun. Then there are the bombings; they happen all over Afghanistan. Only last week eight shepherd boys were slaughtered in a NATO air attack, some only six years old. And the random night raids never stop: families abused in their own homes, children terrified. Everywhere you turn this is happening. *Everywhere!*' Akmed shouts. 'They are destroying Afghanistan!'

He spits, and shakes his fist in the air. But before he can continue, Anoosheh interrupts.

'That may be, cousin,' she says quietly, her voice almost swallowed by the noise of traffic. 'But there are Afghans destroying this country as well, many of them.'

159

Akmed stares incredulously at her. 'What are you talking about?'

'I'm talking about warlords and drug barons who rob us and kill us and tramp all over us.'

'Ah, yes, I agree. But they're working with the unbelievers. They must be expelled, too.'

'Wait.' Anoosheh stops as they reach the top of the lane that leads down to their house, forcing Akmed to do so as well. 'I'm also talking about the Taliban and those who follow them, who seek to ruin our lives.' She stares straight at her cousin. 'I'm talking about women being flogged, and wedding guests beheaded for daring to dance! But you don't see these things, do you, cousin Akmed?'

'No, I don't, because they're not true. They are lies made up by the foreign devils.'

'You're wrong, cousin. Religious extremists commit terrible crimes every day, but you don't see them because you don't want to. You choose to be blind.'

Akmed turns to Naveed and scowls. 'Your sister has developed a loose tongue. You should keep her more—'

'Don't blame my brother for my *loose tongue*. Blame education. It teaches people to think for themselves. But the Taliban and their kind don't want us to think, do they? That's why they bomb schools and murder teachers and throw acid at girls who seek to learn, even shoot them. The power of education frightens the Taliban.'

'Enough, little cousin,' Akmed shouts. 'I know what evil foreigners can do. I know it better than anyone. *They killed my family*.'

'Yes, and I know what evil religious fanatics can do.' Anoosheh shouts back, matching his fury. 'They killed my father and they took away my legs.'

Akmed glares at Anoosheh, his face red, his whole body shaking. She glares back, refusing to be intimidated. Naveed is sandwiched between the two of them, feeling the full force of their combined rage.

'Deny all you wish about the unbelievers!' Akmed hisses. 'But there is one crime they commit which you cannot deny – and it is the worst crime of all.' Akmed brandishes his copy of the Quran. '*They insult Allah!*'

'The worst crime?' Anoosheh replies. 'You—' Before she can go on, a voice calls from the far end of the lane.

'Anoosheh. Naveed.' Their mother is waving to them from the alley outside their house. 'Akmed. Come,' she calls, beckoning frantically. 'At once.'

Naveed squats, letting Anoosheh clamber onto his back. Then he sprints down the lane, followed by Akmed.

Chapter 31

'What is it?' Naveed asks as he reaches his mother.

She is waiting in the outside alcove, her hand on the blanket covering the low doorway.

'Hurry,' she says, drawing the blanket aside and waving them in.

Naveed sets down his sister, handing over her crutches, and together they enter the room with Akmed right behind. Inside, they find Mr Omaid and Jake waiting for them.

There is an uneasy silence, eventually filled by the truck driver.

'Please forgive us for intruding,' he says to Naveed. 'But—'

'Today is a wonderful day, my children,' Naveed's mother cries, pushing past. 'All thanks to your friend.' She points to Jake. 'May Allah shower him with a mountain of blessings. A *wonderful* day.'

'Slow down, Madar, please. What has happened?'

'It's Anoosheh.' She grasps both his hands and laughs out loud. 'Little Noosh!'

'Me?' Anoosheh asks. 'What have I done?'

'It's a miracle.' Her mother throws her arms in the air and then smothers Anoosheh in kisses. 'A miracle!'

Seeing Naveed's and Anoosheh's frustration, Mr Omaid speaks up. 'You were not here when we arrived, so I had to translate as best I could. I hope I have told your mother the right thing, but as you know, my English is very poor. I might have got your friend's message wrong. It was translated by another truck driver at Bagram Airfield.'

'What message?' Naveed shouts in desperation.

'Just tell us!' Anoosheh begs.

'Legs,' Mr Omaid says to her. 'You are to have legs.'

Anoosheh gasps. 'Are you sure?' She looks at Naveed and then turns to Jake, speaking in English. 'Is true?' she whispers. 'I really to have legs?'

Jake nods. 'That's the idea. I got the news only this morning from the doctor in charge of prosthetics at Bagram. Of course, you must realise it will take quite a while. They don't just put new legs on people like that.' He snaps his fingers. 'They need to do tests to make sure it'll work in your case. Measurements have to be taken; casts have to be made, and the legs themselves. Then they need to be fitted and checked, and once that's all okay, you'll have to spend a good while just getting used to them.'

As Naveed listens, the joy builds inside him, watching his sister's face glow.

Jake continues. 'The main point is that you realise the whole thing will take a while. You do understand that, don't you?'

'Yes,' Anoosheh replies, her voice trembling. 'I understand, just cannot believe is happening.'

'Too right it's happening,' Jake says with a chuckle. 'Whenever you're ready.'

'Mr Jake,' Naveed interrupts. 'What you mean, *ready*?'

'The sooner the better. If you guys can come to the air base tomorrow, they'll start the tests straight away. What do you say?'

Anoosheh cannot hold back anymore. 'It's true, Madar,' she shouts in Dari. 'I'm going to have legs!' She rushes forward and throws her arms around her mother, who lifts her up, crying and laughing at the same time. A moment later Naveed joins in, hugging his mother and sister and then spinning them around the room in a swirling dance.

Jake watches them, beaming from ear to ear, and Mr Omaid laughs, clapping and stamping his feet in time as Anoosheh and her mother ululate in celebration. Naveed calls to his cousin and beckons him to join in. But Akmed simply stands there, a blank expression on his face, his eyes staring right through them. Naveed wants to grab his cousin and pull him into the dance. But he's too swept along in the excitement, and by the time he looks around again, Akmed has gone.

Dizzy from spinning and twirling, the dancers eventually stop and Anoosheh wriggles out of her mother's arms. Naveed retrieves her crutches and passes them to her, and together they turn to Jake.

'Thank you,' Anoosheh whispers, tears streaming down her face, 'thank you.'

'No need to thank me, I just made the appointment – that's the easy bit!'

Anoosheh and Naveed shake their heads, thanking Jake over and over until he holds up his hands.

'So does this mean I'll see you all at the base tomorrow morning?' he asks.

'Too rights!' says Anoosheh, grinning through her tears.

Late that night, Naveed sits in the lane outside the house, Nasera's head in his lap. A smile is still on his lips as he thinks about the events of that afternoon and of the great blessings heaped upon him and his family. Anoosheh and his mother chatted well into the evening, long after Jake and Mr Omaid left, unable to sleep with all the excitement. He has thanked Allah many times for sending Mr Jake into their lives, but does so again with a silent prayer as he gazes up at the stars.

There is a sad note to the day, though, which he can't push away – Akmed. Naveed is angry with himself for not chasing after his cousin when he walked out that afternoon. He so wanted Akmed to be part of their happiness, to join in their joy. He should never have let him go. But he did, and now his cousin may well have gone forever.

He understands Akmed's feelings; losing his whole family that way would have to leave the deepest of scars. He understands Akmed's outrage about the burning of the Quran, too. What Muslim wouldn't be outraged? He understands the anger and the urge for revenge as well. These are natural emotions in the face of such crimes. But Naveed knows that they are not good emotions; you cannot build anything on them. They only grow more of the same.

Earlier that afternoon when Akmed and Anoosheh were arguing, Naveed could feel his cousin's anger and hatred like a physical force, a wall. He wanted to say something then. He wanted to tell Akmed that there was a better way, one with tolerance and understanding. But his cousin would not have listened – he was far too incensed – and then the opportunity passed. Now it would probably never arise again.

Naveed peers up the lane, hoping Akmed will appear. 'Where is he?' he whispers, gently stroking Nasera – waiting, wishing.

After a while he stands. He leads Nasera to her basket and puts her to bed. But then, as he is about to enter the house he hears his father's voice.

Never despair. Tomorrow is a new—

Yes, Padar, I know – a new day that brings new light. Don't worry, I haven't forgotten your words: I will always seek the light.

Chapter 32

'He's forgotten.'

'No, Madar. He would never forget.'

'Nonsense, Naveed. Men forget everything. You forgot to wake up this morning.'

'I did not forget to wake up.'

'You did so. I had to shake you awake.'

'Yes, I know, long before sunrise. Because you couldn't sleep we had to sit around for hours.'

'Well, there's no point in being late.'

'Don't worry, Madar, there is no chance of that.'

Naveed is waiting with his mother and sister for Mr Omaid. Last night he agreed he'd take them to Bagram Airfield in the morning, in his truck, arranging to pick them up at the top of the lane that leads from their house.

'Oh dear.' Naveed's mother suddenly thrusts her hand to her mouth. 'Perhaps *we're* late,' she shrieks. 'Do you think Mr Omaid has given up waiting for us and gone?'

'Please!' Anoosheh shouts. 'Stop it!'

'What?' Her mother looks surprised. 'Stop what?'

Anoosheh leans on her crutches, frowning. 'Worrying, stressing, fretting. Please stop, Madar. You're making us all nervous.'

'Yes, but if Mr Omaid has—'

'Madar!' Anoosheh growls this time, surprising Naveed as well. 'Mr Omaid has not gone, and he is not late. We are early, that's all. *Very, very* early. So please sit down.'

'Very well. As you wish.' Her mother sniffs and perches on the edge of a low rock wall. 'Have it your way.' She fidgets with her scarf for a little while. 'But if we're—'

'Shush!' Both Naveed and Anoosheh pounce on her this time.

She recoils at once. 'My lips are sealed,' she says, holding a finger up to her mouth.

Naveed leans down and pats Nasera. His mother looks askance at the animal and huffs.

'Why is the dog coming to the hospital?' she asks, drumming her fingers on the wall.

'Mr Jake asked me to bring her, Madar. Who knows? Maybe he has some good news for her as well.'

'Very funny.' She turns away and searches the traffic.

'Here he is,' Anoosheh shouts.

Mr Omaid's brightly decorated jingle truck slips out of the heavy traffic and pulls up in front of them. 'Sorry I'm late,' he says, climbing down from the cabin.

'A breakdown on the road.' He throws his arms in the air. 'Come, all aboard.'

He leads them around to the passenger's side, helping Anoosheh into the cabin and lending a hand to her mother. Naveed goes to the back of the truck, lifts Nasera on and is about to clamber up himself when Akmed appears from the lane and walks towards him.

'Wait, Mr Omaid,' Naveed calls. 'Madar. Look who it is.'

A cry of delight bursts from the cabin. 'He has come back,' Naveed's mother exclaims. 'Thanks be to Allah.'

'Are you all right?' Naveed asks as Akmed reaches him. His cousin's face is ashen, his eyes sunken, dark shadows under them, while the bulky black coat he wears makes him appear even paler. And smaller; it is far too big for him. 'You look terrible.'

Akmed ignores Naveed's comment. 'I want to come with you.'

'Of course. No one is more welcome. Let me help you up.' Naveed reaches out to him.

'I'm fine,' Akmed replies, grabbing at the rail. His hand is shaking and his grip looks weak.

'But cousin, I can see you're not—'

'I said, I'm fine,' Akmed snaps. 'A little tired, that's all. Leave me be.'

Naveed stands back while his cousin climbs aboard, then follows.

'You've brought the dog,' Akmed complains as soon as Naveed is on the truck.

'Yes. My friend asked me to. We—'

'That dog doesn't like me. Look how he stares at me.'

'She, Akmed. Nasera's a female. And you're wrong – she does like you. See, she's sniffing you again, as before.'

'Yes. Getting ready to bite, I'm sure. Keep her away from me.' Akmed steps warily around Nasera and hurries to the front of the truck. But she tags him, continuing to sniff. 'Keep her away, I said!'

Naveed clips a leash onto Nasera's collar, and ties her up at his side, well away from Akmed. Even so, his cousin still fidgets, increasing the gap between them. Naveed wants to say something, but decides to leave it for the moment. Perhaps the drive and some fresh air will improve things. He taps the roof and calls out to Mr Omaid. The truck clunks into gear and trundles off.

The drive actually makes things worse. It is slow and tedious, the traffic endlessly stopping and starting. This makes Akmed even more edgy. He huffs and sighs, glancing behind or craning his neck to peer ahead. Naveed can feel the tension coming from his cousin, and decides that he has to speak up.

'What's wrong, Akmed?'

'Nothing, I tell you. Nothing. Why won't you believe me?'

'Because I'm not blind. You're shaking, you're as pale as a ghost, you look as if you haven't slept all night and you're so on edge.'

Akmed moderates his tone a little at this. 'I'm sorry if I'm jumpy. I don't mean to be. I had a bad night.

Thinking, you know? Lots of thinking. Allah helped me search my soul.'

'I guessed as much,' Naveed replies, trying to sound understanding. 'At least you decided to come back to us. I'm glad of that.' His cousin shrugs at this but doesn't reply. 'So where did you sleep last night?'

'I don't know,' Akmed mutters. 'In a doorway some-where, I think.'

'It must have been freezing.'

Akmed only grunts.

'Lucky you had that coat.'

'Coat?' Akmed glares at Naveed. 'What about the coat?'

'Aram shoo – calm down.' Naveed backs off, shocked at the wildness in his cousin's eyes. 'I only meant how lucky you were to have the coat last night. To keep you warm.'

'Warm?' Akmed scowls. 'Yes, I suppose so,' he adds, then looks away. They have reached the outskirts of Bagram Airfield. He peers ahead and nods. 'Not long now,' he says, as much to himself as anyone.

Naveed doesn't need to look ahead. He knows exactly where they are. They've just entered the narrow avenue leading to Entry Control Point One, about to join the long queue of trucks slowly weaving around blast blocks and over speed bumps. He's seen the queues before and knows that this part of the trip will take a while. That doesn't worry him at all. It's his cousin that he's concerned about. There is definitely something very odd about him.

Naveed can't stop thinking about Akmed's sudden outburst over his coat, of all things! Why would he get so worked up by something like that? It doesn't make sense.

Unless . . .

Naveed stares at Akmed and a chilling thought slowly creeps up on him. He stares at his cousin's shaking hands, at his face and neck wet with sweat, at his lips now moving rapidly as if talking to himself. No, he's praying – his cousin is praying. Finally Naveed stares at the big bulky coat that at first just made Akmed look a bit comical. And gradually – terrifyingly – he understands what he is staring at.

A suicide bomber.

Cousin Akmed is a suicide bomber!

Chapter 33

Naveed breaks into a cold sweat. Impossible, he tells himself. Ridiculous. He must be imagining it. But then Nasera tugs at her leash, straining to get closer to Akmed, and all the doubt instantly vanishes.

How could he have been so blind? So stupid? That's why Nasera was sniffing Akmed in the lane that night – she could smell the residue of explosives on him. And now she can smell the *bomb* on him, wrapped around his body, no doubt, packed into the lining of that coat.

This nightmare is real, and Naveed is right in the middle of it. So are his mother and sister. And Mr Omaid. At the very least he has to get them as far away as possible. But how? Akmed is so tense that any sudden move, anything to raise suspicion might tip him over the edge.

Naveed's throat is bone dry, his head spinning, and he feels as if he'll faint at any moment.

'What are you staring at?'

He only just hears his cousin's voice, for it is almost drowned out by the wave of panic washing over him. He grips the railing to steady himself.

'What's wrong with you?' Akmed shouts.

'Sorry, cousin,' Naveed replies. Urging himself to keep calm, he takes a deep breath, trying to think what to say next. 'I was daydreaming. It's so slow, getting into the base. I just drifted off and was staring into space.'

'What's all the delay?'

'Inspections. Papers, vehicles, people. But they're mainly checking for, er, bombs.' Naveed stumbles over the word, hoping his cousin won't notice.

'Does that mean they will inspect us?' The note of alarm in Akmed's voice is unmistakable.

'Yes,' Naveed replies, watching his cousin closely. 'I expect so.'

'But I thought your friend would let us through. Surely he knows you wouldn't be carrying a bomb.'

Suddenly Naveed has an idea. Like a chink of light at the end of a dark tunnel, he sees a chance to get his family and Mr Omaid away from Akmed. He peers ahead and can just see Mr Jake at the entry control point.

'You're right,' he says. 'Good thinking, Akmed. I'll send Madar and Anoosheh up to the main gate. Mr Jake is expecting them. He'll then call us through in the truck.'

Before Akmed can reply, Naveed scrambles over the side of the truck, and pulls open the passenger's door.

'Come along, you two,' he calls to his mother and sister. 'We could be stuck here forever. Mr Jake is keen to get you in for those tests, Noosh, and it will be much faster if you walk up to him.'

Mr Omaid is already at Naveed's side. 'Good idea,' he says, helping Anoosheh and her mother down from the cabin.

'Hurry up,' Naveed adds, handing Anoosheh her crutches. He walks a little way with them, until they're out of Akmed's earshot. Then he turns to his sister. 'I want you to give Mr Jake a message. Tell him that Nasera has found something big, *very* big. Is that clear?'

Anoosheh frowns. 'Is something the m—'

'No time for questions. The doctor will be waiting to start on your legs.' Naveed stares into her eyes. 'Just do as I ask: make sure you give Mr Jake my message.'

Anoosheh nods and heads off with her mother. Naveed watches them go, wishing he could hug and hold them close, but knowing better. His mother would sense his anxiety and instantly become suspicious.

'We should get through now,' he calls to Akmed as he walks back to the truck. His cousin is watching him closely. 'Anoosheh will work her magic on the foreigners to get us into the base.' He laughs but feels sick with worry.

Mr Omaid has the bonnet of the truck up, checking the engine's oil and water. Naveed joins him and presses close.

'Do this for me now,' he whispers. 'I beg of you. Tell the driver in front to move, and the one behind. Then you must also get as far away from here as possible.'

175

Mr Omaid's face drops. 'What . . .? God forbid! Don't tell me your cousin—'

'Please!' Naveed hisses. 'Any delay could be fatal.'

'But what of you, my boy?'

'I will go to Akmed. With God's help I will change his mind.'

'Don't be crazy. You mustn't—'

'No, Mr Omaid.' Naveed holds up his hands. 'I *must*. My cousin has no one else. I cannot leave him alone.'

He turns and walks away, uttering a quick prayer under his breath as he climbs onto the back of the truck.

'What's the matter?' Akmed demands, nodding at the open bonnet. 'We're not broken down, I hope.'

'Not at all, cousin. Mr Omaid just needs a little water for the engine. He's going to see if any of the other drivers have some.' Naveed peers ahead. 'Aha, Noosh and Madar have nearly reached Mr Jake. We should be on our way soon.'

Naveed is struggling with his emotions, a whole mix of them churning inside him. He kneels down and pats Nasera, hoping that might give him time to think. She nudges into him with a soft whining noise, as if sensing his anguish. He pulls her close and hugs her hard, aware that he may never do this again.

For a moment he loses himself in that simple act, to the point where everything else becomes unimportant. A strange calm folds around him like a bubble of peace. That's when he hears the voice.

'Say no to violence.'

He knows exactly who it is, Malalai Farzana. He's heard her say those words before. She never gives up calling on Afghans to unite in peace. At first Naveed thinks the voice is only in his head – that he's hearing things. But then he realises it is coming from a radio.

'Say no to vengeance and hatred.'

A radio somewhere, almost certainly in one of the jingle trucks. She is faint, and Naveed has to listen hard to hear her. But as he does so, he is struck by a simple truth. He's not the only one listening to Malalai. Another Afghan is, a truck driver somewhere. And there would be others, too, elsewhere, all over the country – truck drivers, shopkeepers, doctors, teachers, farmers, men, women and children. There must be Afghans everywhere listening to this call for peace. Listening and hoping.

'Seek better ways to solve differences – through talking, not fighting; with words, not weapons.'

'What's going on?'

Naveed is shaken from his thoughts by Akmed's angry voice. He looks up and at once sees the blind hate burning in his cousin's eyes. But then he sees more – fear, confusion, maybe even a cry for help – and realises that whatever else his cousin might be, in essence he's just a frightened young man who has lost his way.

'The truck behind us is moving away. And the one in front. What's happening?'

Akmed's voice is shrill with suspicion, but Naveed doesn't let that worry him. He feels a quiet strength deep inside himself. Malalai Farzana has given that to him. With her words fixed in his mind he slowly stands:

'They're probably sick of waiting,' he replies.

But the trucks leave in a hurry, their tyres screeching. One of the drivers glares out his window at them as he passes.

'They seem to be in a big rush,' Akmed snaps. 'Maybe Mr Omaid said something to them.'

'What do you mean?' Naveed laughs. 'What would he say to them, Akmed?'

He glances towards the entry control point, relieved to see that his mother and sister are being bustled away. But Akmed sees this, too, and, like Naveed, also sees that Jake is talking to an officer, both glancing in the direction of the cousins. Almost immediately a stream of soldiers fan out, deploying themselves behind blast blocks and Hesco bags. Some already have their guns aimed in the truck's direction. A turtleback Humvee pulls out of the entry control area and begins creeping towards them.

'Stop pretending,' Akmed says. 'You know exactly what Mr Omaid said to them.'

Naveed can feel Akmed's glare on him. He faces his cousin squarely, and nods. 'Yes, I do know. I had to stop you going ahead with this madness.'

'That won't stop me,' Akmed shouts, pulling a mobile phone from his coat pocket. 'I only have to press a button, any button.'

Naveed watches as his cousin's finger hovers over the phone, shaking perilously close to it. 'Why are you doing this, Akmed?'

'For Allah, of course. To make the foreign devils pay for their blasphemy, and any Afghan traitors who would support them.'

'But this won't hurt any foreigners, Akmed. Look, they're all safe. It won't even hurt your Afghan traitors, except for me. Apart from that, you'll only blow up Mr Omaid's truck and put a big hole in the ground.'

Akmed shakes his head, not wanting to listen.

'It won't serve any purpose,' Naveed continues. 'It won't be jihad. It will only be one sad young man killing himself and a cousin who was stupid enough to stay by his side because he cares. You'll also break the hearts of two other people who care for you and love you as well, my sister and mother. Don't for a minute think that Allah will give you a place in Paradise for this. Yours will be just one more wasted life in this futile war. Is that really what you want, Akmed?'

'Ha, very smart of you, cousin. But I have no choice now. Look at the Americans, they have their guns aimed, ready to kill me. And if by some miracle they do not, I will be a prisoner, locked up in Parwan forever.'

'They will not kill you, Akmed, but it is true, they will take you in. And they will interrogate you, yes. But I don't think it will be nearly as bad as you believe if you surrender to them. And whatever happens, cousin, you will not be alone. I promise that I and my mother and sister will stand by you.'

'And I also promise.'

Akmed and Naveed jump, and turn around to find Mr Omaid standing behind them.

'Not only that,' he continues. 'If you hand over the phone now, I will promise you a job and place to live if you want them when you do come out of Parwan Prison. My business has been doing well and I plan to buy a second truck. So I will need a driver. What do you say?'

Akmed is completely lost for words.

So is Naveed. All he can do is gape at Mr Omaid, who would never have been his idea of a hero. And yet here he is risking his life to offer not just compassion but understanding and *real* support. And he's not asking anything in return. He's giving.

'Well, young man?' Mr Omaid holds out his hand to Akmed for the mobile phone. 'Do we have a deal?'

Akmed stares down at the device in his hand.

Naveed holds his breath as the world seems to come to a halt. Mr Omaid gazes steadily at Akmed, his arm outstretched motionless before him.

Akmed's eyes are locked on the phone; the shaking of his hand is the only thing that disturbs the air around them. Then, very slowly, he blinks.

Without taking his eyes off the phone, Akmed passes it to Mr Omaid.

As soon as he does so, Naveed steps forward and embraces his cousin. Mr Omaid holds up the phone for the soldiers to see, and a loud cheer erupts from the entry control point.

Jake clambers onto a concrete blast block so that Naveed can see him, and punches the air in a victory salute.

Chapter 34

An hour later the crisis is over and Akmed has been taken away, but Naveed's mind is still churning.

He sits on the running board of Mr Omaid's truck, his head in his hands, still tense as can be. It is partly a kind of delayed reaction from the stress of dealing with his cousin. Yet it is also more. He's annoyed with himself for not having asked a question of Akmed before they took him away. But then he's fairly sure he knows the answer.

'Well done.' Jake appears and sits beside Naveed, slapping a reassuring hand on his shoulder. 'You're a hero, mate. Kabul is sending a TV crew to interview you and Mr Omaid. You'll be famous.'

Naveed looks up, not really having heard what Jake said. 'I should have talk Akmed before soldiers take him,' he says.

'Hey, don't worry about Akmed. They'll be fair with him. You need to relax now. It's all over.'

'No, Mr Jake. Is not all over. It just start.'

'What do you mean?'

'I think I know where Akmed get bomb. He not work alone.'

'Are you sure?'

Naveed nods. 'Yes. And sure there is more bomb. Lot more. We must go now.'

Jake leaps up and sends an urgent call straight through to Unit Command.

'Request GAF for urgent off-base mission.'

Within twenty minutes the ground assault force Jake requested arrives in the warehouse district where Naveed lives. Four turtlebacks take up tactical positions, isolating the streets and buildings in the area. All exits are sealed off and the troops move in.

'I hope your hunch is right,' Jake says as he and Naveed step out of their Humvee with Stingray and Nasera on leashes. There is a worried expression in his eyes, but he grins at Naveed and gives him the thumbs up. 'Lead on, mate.'

They head straight to the top of the lane that goes to Naveed's house. There they wait for a moment. A reconnaissance squad has gone ahead to make sure all is clear and has taken up its position outside Mr Kalin's warehouse. As soon as the A-OK is given, Jake and Naveed set off down the lane to join the squad. Naveed clenches his fists as they walk, his heart thumping loudly.

'Please, Allah, I know I am right in this,' he whispers. 'But we might need some help.'

When they reach the reconnaissance squad and turn into the parking bay, Naveed gulps. Two vehicles are outside the warehouse. He immediately recognises them. One is Mr Kalin's, the other belongs to Salar Khan, the drug lord. Both men appear at the door of the warehouse. Salar Khan mutters something and quickly steps back into the warehouse. Mr Kalin walks over to the soldiers.

'What's all this about?' he demands, his words translated to the commanding officer by an interpreter. 'What's going on?'

'We have reason to believe that explosives may be stored in this warehouse,' the officer replies.

'Explosives? Don't be ridiculous. I'm a respectable merchant. I have a position in this community. How can you think I would—'

'We have reliable information, that's all I can say,' the officer adds.

Mr Kalin glares at Naveed. 'You mean the boy? Ha. He's nothing but a liar. You can't take his word against mine.'

'I'm sorry but we are going to search your warehouse. If you choose to resist we will have no alternative but to use force. Is that understood?'

Mr Kalin bristles with anger. 'You are the one who will be sorry. Let me make it very clear that when you find nothing – and believe me, you *will* find nothing – I will take this to the very top and your head will be the first to roll.'

'That's a risk I'll have to take,' the commanding officer replies, and motions to his men. 'We do this by the book, guys. Handle everything with care. No rough stuff, no breakages.'

As soon as the soldiers file into the warehouse they gape at the task ahead of them. The area undercover is vast, perhaps two acres, all of it packed to the limit with goods and stores. Bags of grain are piled right up to the high ceiling; containers of tinned and dried food stacked upon each other in long rows that disappear into the dark depths of the warehouse. Timber and steel and other building materials are loaded precariously on pallets, along with bags of cement and lime, as well as tins of paint and drums of chemicals.

'Where the hell do you start?' the commanding officer groans. He looks around, scratching his head. 'Do your best, guys,' he says eventually, sending the men off. The soldiers fan out through the warehouse.

Progress is slow and tedious, made doubly difficult by the extreme narrowness of the aisles. In their bulky gear the soldiers can only just fit down most of the passageways. In some cases they can't even turn around, and are forced to back out.

The search is no easier for Jake and Naveed. The warehouse is swirling with all sorts of smells – chemicals of every type, paints, herbicides, detergents, diesel and oil, along with grains and other foodstuffs. This heady mix overloads the dogs' sense of smell, making it very difficult for them to focus. Stingray is completely confused and has already lost interest, but Nasera is still trying. Naveed is sure that given time she will grow used to the many smells and be able to do her job properly. But time is quickly evaporating.

And then the commanding officer's order comes for all the troops to cease operations.

'Hear that?' Jake yells to Naveed. The two of them are searching in aisles parallel to each other. 'They're calling off the search.'

'No, Mr Jake. Not stop now. I sure we close.'

'Sorry, but orders are orders. We have to obey them.'

Reluctantly Naveed turns Nasera around and joins Jake. They walk back to meet up with the rest of the squad near the front of the warehouse. Mr Kalin is talking to the commanding officer, a smirk on his face. He stands in front of a huge pile of agricultural chemicals in containers stacked high on pallets.

'What did I tell you?' he says to the commanding officer through the interpreter. 'But I am a fair man. I know you are only doing your job. So I will not press charges, provided you leave now.' He glares at Naveed. 'You will not be so fortunate!'

Naveed flares up. 'I know what I saw that night,' he shouts, stepping towards Mr Kalin, Nasera straining at the end of her leash. 'I know you're hiding—'

'Are you crazy?' Mr Kalin shouts. 'Keep that dog away from me!'

'Stop!' the commanding officer yells at Naveed. 'Restrain your dog at once.'

But Nasera breaks free and leaps forward, knocking Mr Kalin to the ground.

'Komak! Help!' he screams, shielding himself from the dog.

Several soldiers hurry to his assistance, but there is no need. Nasera is not interested in Mr Kalin. She has her snout pressed hard at the base of a pallet, sniffing frantically and trying to dig under it.

'Look at her!' Naveed shouts.

Jake immediately lets Stingray go. The kelpie runs straight to Nasera's side and begins sniffing and scratching as well.

'I think we might be onto something,' he says to the commanding officer. 'I'd love to see what's under those pallets.'

The dogs are pulled back and a forklift is brought in, despite Mr Kalin's protests. The pallets are then shifted one by one. It's a slow process for there are many of them, but eventually the area is cleared to reveal a cement floor covered by a light layer of dirt. Naveed's heart sinks.

'See,' Mr Kalin snaps. 'Solid cement.' He turns on the commanding officer, his face flushed with anger. 'Now you will leave!' he says, pointing to the door. 'Go!'

'Not so fast,' Jake calls. He grabs a broom and sweeps back some of the dirt. A fine line is just visible in the cement. More dirt is swept away. 'This looks like a trapdoor to me.'

The commanding officer steps closer and studies the cement floor, then motions for Jake to continue. When the area is swept properly two soldiers lever the trapdoor open.

The commanding officer shines his torch down into the hole. 'My God,' he gasps, as the beam illuminates a vast underground cavern filled with weapons and explosives, more than enough to supply a small army. 'Look what we've just found.'

'And look what we found.'

There's a scuffle at the entrance to the warehouse. Two more soldiers appear with Salar Khan handcuffed between them.

'We caught him trying to escape down a back lane. We thought he might be part of the problem.'

Naveed laughs. 'You bloody right,' he adds in English. 'He biggest part of problem.'

Chapter 35

'**Zemestan khalas shud – winter** is finished – fellow Afghans. Spring is with us.'

Naveed sits outside the base hospital at Bagram Airfield, listening to Malalai Farzana on a small hand-crank radio, a gift from Mr Jake. Nasera lies next to him. He reaches down and pats her.

'Not too much longer,' he whispers, glancing towards the main doors of the hospital.

He's waiting for Anoosheh. He's been waiting quite a while, but is happy to sit there for as long as it takes, knowing that the end result will be well worth it.

'Let us follow nature's example,' Malalai Farzana continues. 'Let us end our long winter of war. Let us chase it from our land once and for all. Let us replace it with a bright new spring of hope.'

The radio lies in Naveed's lap. He treasures it dearly and listens to it every night – that is, if his sister hasn't grabbed it first. He listens through the day, too – that is, if his mother hasn't taken it.

'And we *can* make it happen, brothers and sisters, as long as each of us does our bit. Together we can do it!'

Malalai Farzana is spreading her message of peace and unity and hope. Naveed is sure there are other Afghans doing just the same as him, for she often broadcasts now, and they say her following grows each day.

He has heard her several times now on the little radio, and each time it almost feels as if she's talking directly to him. Ever since that day with Cousin Akmed on the back of Mr Omaid's truck, he has felt a powerful personal connection to her words.

Say no to violence. Say no to vengeance and hatred. Seek better ways to solve differences – through talking, not fighting; with words, not weapons.

They were her words that day. He remembers them coming from a radio somewhere, and they have never left his thoughts.

Naveed pulls Nasera closer and gives her a hug. 'You did your bit that day,' he tells her. 'You saved many lives by stopping Akmed. And later, at Mr Kalin's warehouse. Many lives.'

That discovery was extremely important, Jake later explained to Naveed. A major attack on Bagram Airfield had been planned to take place soon after the riots over the Quran burnings. Salar Khan was to supply the weapons and explosives for the attack from the huge stockpile hidden beneath Mr Kalin's warehouse. It would have been a disaster for the Americans – a disaster for everyone, in fact. Casualties on both sides would have been enormous, the causes of peace and democracy dealt a fatal blow.

'Mr Jake says I deserve a medal for that,' Naveed tells Nasera. 'But we both know who really deserves a medal, eh?' He rubs her vigorously all over. 'You're the real hero.'

Besides, Naveed has taken away things from that day that are far more important than any medal.

He discovered a personal strength he never realised he had, when he decided to stay with Cousin Akmed. He learned of courage and selflessness, too, when Mr Omaid joined them on the back of the truck. With those two simple acts, something truly important happened to Naveed. *Weakness, fear and hopelessness died. Strength, power and courage were born.* Naveed saw that he – a boy – could make a difference, that he really did have a part to play in the future of his country.

Naveed also made a true friend that day, in Mr Omaid, someone he not only likes but respects as well. The whole family does. The funny little round man often visits them, bringing treats and laughter. He's won Anoosheh's heart with his magic tricks, and made their mother laugh on many occasions. Nasera likes him, too.

And then there's Pari. *Dear Pari.* With Salar Khan imprisoned, her nightmare of marriage to the cruel old man was suddenly over. Naveed has seen her often since then, and his heart rejoices at how her face glows again as it once used to.

So much good has come to them, Naveed thinks,

since Nasera and Mr Omaid and Mr Jake came into their lives. He feels a wave of warmth for the young Australian – without Mr Jake none of this would have happened. He saw Nasera's potential and developed it. He organised all the paperwork for Naveed and Nasera to get into the explosive detection course, along with a recommendation from his boss. And he made Anoosheh's legs happen.

But that's not all. Over the last few weeks Mr Jake has worked tirelessly on Akmed's behalf, persuading the Americans that he is not a bad person, just a troubled young man preyed upon by jihadists. Mr Omaid has helped as well; he has gone guarantor for Akmed and promised him work as a truck driver when he is freed. That will not happen for a while yet, but at least Akmed now has hope for a better future.

'Hey, Navvy.'

Naveed spins around. Mr Jake is jogging up Disney Drive, Stingray at his side. Nasera immediately bounds off. When she reaches the Australian, he hurls two balls into the air and the dogs chase after them. As Naveed laughs at their antics, he hears Malalai Farzana concluding her speech on the radio.

'It will be a long struggle, fellow Afghans, make no mistake. It will be a long journey. But if we stand together, if we walk as one, if we help each other along the way, we will get there. *We will!*'

He nods in agreement, turning off the radio just as Jake joins him.

'Don't tell me Anoosheh isn't out yet?'

Naveed throws his hands in the air. 'Long time waiting, Mr Jake, loooong time waiting.'

'Yeah, well, that's women for you, mate. Get used to it,' he says with a comical grin as he sits down beside Naveed.

That grin makes Naveed want to laugh. But at the same time a shadow of sadness drifts over him. For he knows in his heart that Mr Jake will leave Afghanistan soon; his contract will finish and he will have to go, as most of the foreigners will. Naveed knows that this is how it must be. Malalai Farzana has been telling him so for a long time.

We Afghans must govern ourselves without foreigners holding our hand. It is our only way forward.

Yet all the knowing in the world will never fill the hole left when his friend does eventually go.

'What's the matter?' Jake asks, seeing the sadness in Naveed's eyes. 'You okay?'

Naveed lowers his gaze. 'You good man, Mr Jake,' he says, fighting back the tears. 'You most good man.' He keeps his eyes on the ground, but the tremble in his voice gives him away.

'Hey, little mate,' Jake says. 'What's with the sadness? You should be happy. This is happy hour.'

Naveed nods vigorously. He wants to tell Mr Jake that you can be happy and sad at the same time, but the words stick in his throat. It doesn't matter, though, because when he looks up he sees that Mr Jake understands. Naveed smiles back at his friend, but before he can say anything, the hospital doors burst open. His mother comes rushing out.

'Ayee,' she cries. 'Look at my daughter, my beautiful daughter.'

Seconds later Anoosheh appears in the doorway. She steadies herself on the railing for a moment, staring across at Naveed.

'Look at me, brother,' she says, her voice trembling.

Naveed cannot do anything else *but* look at his sister. He cannot take his eyes off her, barely able to believe that the girl standing before him is the same one who entered the hospital that morning. She's so new and different, so tall and proud.

She wears a new perahan toombon bought especially for this occasion – a blue outfit, the blue of lapis lazuli, with gold trimming on the shirt and trousers. Special shoes provided by Dr Radcliffe poke out from beneath the trousers. Her face glows. Her eyes sparkle. All Naveed can do is gape, sure he will burst with the joy bubbling inside.

Anoosheh lets go of the railing, walks over to her brother and throws her arms around him. They hug silently, words completely out of place.

Their mother joins them, wrapping them in her arms, and in that moment, Naveed knows that his father is there as well. He can feel him, larger than life, folded around them all. And he can hear him.

In every darkness there is light. Always look for the light.

A giant troop carrier thunders down the runway and up into a cloudless blue. Its roar is deafening, but Naveed only hears his father.

The darker it gets, the harder you must seek.

His eyes follow the mighty metal bird as it rises over the Shomali Plain towards the mountains of the Hindu Kush. But his spirits have already risen higher still.

You are right, Padar. The world lives on hope.

Author's note

More than thirty years ago I spent time in Afghanistan. My wife and I were on a six-month overland trip to Europe through Asia and the Middle East using local transport. I now realise that the seeds for *Naveed* were in fact planted then. I was spellbound by Afghanistan, its people, its culture and history. I tried to return in the mid-eighties, when travelling alone through Uzbekistan and Tajikistan, but by then the country was embroiled in a fierce war with Russia that lasted a decade, leaving an estimated two million Afghans dead and almost as many disabled. The war didn't end there, though; like a cancer it grew into another decade, and another.

For me, Afghanistan is a treasure-chest of indelible experiences. Take the Buddhas of Bamiyan, for instance, two huge statues (one 53 metres high, the other 35) carved into cliffs about 230 kilometres north-west of Kabul. On the outskirts of tiny Bamiyan, our truck was stopped by a soldier standing on a raised platform at a roundabout, hand up, blowing a whistle, rifle ready. His uniform was tattered and ill-fitting, he had no shoes, and his firearm was actually made of wood. We were the only vehicle on the road, not even a cart and donkey within cooee. But the little traffic controller double-checked that all was clear before whistling and waving us on. Later that afternoon we sat on top of the Buddhas and stared out over fertile flood plains that stretched forever.

We were wrapped in a rich cloak of history, yet I found myself thinking about the little traffic controller who took his job so seriously.

In March 2001 the Taliban destroyed the Buddhas with dynamite. When I saw those ancient statues blown to bits, I wept for the great loss of history and culture in that brutal, mindless moment. But I also wept for the little traffic controller, for I knew that his whole world had been blown to bits as well. That's what the beast of war does. In part I've written this book for people like him, a book which has in fact been brewing in me for years.

Politicians love reminding us that war is about courage and heroism and acts beyond the call of duty. But without diminishing our soldiers' role in Afghanistan, I knew I had to write about the little people in that war – women and children, widows and orphans, the injured and maimed. I wanted to write as well about those who seek to mend the shattered lives that war spews out – doctors, teachers, aid workers, ordinary men and women – those who try to build something from the rubble and ruin. To me all these little people are in fact huge people. In researching *Naveed*, I found real rays of hope in the individual stories of men, women and children, real grounds for optimism in the way Afghans are helping Afghans climb out of their nightmare. They are the real heroes of the war in Afghanistan, with stories more uplifting and inspiring than you can ever imagine.

A small but vital example. In researching the subject of Arms and Explosives Search (AES) dogs, I came upon the MDC – the Mine Detection Centre – which operates out of Kabul. Landmines, roadside bombs and IEDs are among the biggest killers in Afghanistan. In the first half of 2012, for instance, almost 1200 Afghan civilians were killed and 2000 wounded by them. The MDC is operated by Afghans, and runs an eighteen-month program that trains dogs and their owners in explosives detection. This program is not just about transforming dogs into highly skilled mine detectors; it's about helping Afghans make a real difference in a country that is among the top three most mined on the planet.

There is a growing realisation among Afghans that they alone can rebuild their country. And as the West prepares to walk away from the mess it helped create, the importance of that realisation is greater than ever.

'It will be a long struggle,' says Malalai Joya, that immensely brave woman, the Voice of the Voiceless. 'But if we can unite for justice and democracy, our people will be like a flood that no one can stop.'

Only the little people can prove her right.

Timeline

1919 Third Anglo-Afghan War: Kingdom of Afghanistan gains independence from Britain.

1933 King Mohammed Zahir Shah begins four-decade reign.

1950s Afghanistan develops close ties with Soviet Union during Cold War.

1973 Shah overthrown and Democratic Republic of Afghanistan established.

1978 Saur Revolution: People's Democratic Party of Afghanistan (PDPA) seizes power in a pro-Soviet communist coup and installs socialist agenda. Islamic militant groups known as Mujaheddin build resistance in country regions.

1979–1989 Soviet War in Afghanistan: PDPA requests support of Soviet Union against Mujaheddin resistance. 100 000 Red Army troops enter Afghanistan. Thousands of refugees flee to Iran and Pakistan.

1989 Soviet troops withdraw. Estimated 2 million Afghan people dead, 1.5 million disabled. Infighting continues as US, Pakistan and Saudi

Arabia support Mujaheddin's attempts to oust communist government.

1989–1992 Afghan Civil War: Soviet-backed government collapses; Peshawar Accord establishes Islamic State of Afghanistan but civil war follows as Islamic warlords vie for control.

1994–1996 Islamic militant group the Taliban seizes control of Kandahar and Kabul and sets up Islamic Emirate of Afghanistan. Enforces law and order through civilian massacres and strict interpretation of Sharia law. Osama bin Laden, leader of international terrorist group al-Qaeda, finances the Taliban and sets up training camps in Afghanistan.

1998 Taliban consolidates control over northern and western Afghanistan. Estimated 4000 civilians executed at Mazar-i-Sharif as Taliban targets Shiite Hazaras.

2001 Ahmad Shah Masood, leader of the Northern Alliance, main opposition to the Taliban, is assassinated by al-Qaeda. On 11 September four US airliners are hijacked and used in terrorist strikes on the World Trade Center and Pentagon. More than 3000 killed.

War in Afghanistan: The US and its allies launch military operations in Afghanistan. Operation Enduring Freedom dismantles al-Qaeda and removes the Taliban, who refuse to hand over Osama bin Laden. Allied forces and the anti-Taliban Northern Alliance recapture major cities and towns. Taliban regime collapses and leaders retreat to remote mountains and Pakistan.

Bonn Agreement: Prominent Afghans meet to re-create the government of Afghanistan. The United Nations Security Council, with the support of the Northern Alliance, installs Hamid Karzai as interim administration head and establishes the International Security Assistance Force (ISAF) to oversee security and train Afghan National Army.

2002 Interim government in Kabul is established. Bagram Airfield becomes main base for US forces.

2003 North Atlantic Treaty Organisation (NATO) assumes leadership of ISAF and deploys first contingent of foreign peacekeepers from 49 countries. Taliban and al-Qaeda regroup to launch renewed 'jihad'.

2004 Afghans vote in first parliamentary elections in more than thirty years. Hamid Karzai assumes Presidency of Islamic Republic of Afghanistan.

2006–2009 NATO countries pledge to increase military and civilian support to Afghanistan. US troop numbers boosted to almost 100 000. Hamid Karzai sworn in for a second term as president.

2010 NATO agrees to hand control of security to Afghan forces by end of 2014. Insurgent attacks peak at estimated 1500; almost 10 000 people killed.

2011 Battle of Kandahar: Major offensive strike by Taliban. US forces kill Osama bin Laden in Pakistan. US and NATO countries begin to withdraw troops. President Karzai negotiates a ten-year partnership with the US to retain some US troops post 2014.

2012 Violent protests follow burning of copies of the Quran by US soldiers at Bagram Airfield. Estimated thirty people killed and more than 200 wounded.

2013 US continues its training and advisory role as NATO hands over security to estimated 350 000 Afghan forces. ISAF gives control of last 95 districts to Afghan forces. Australia announces withdrawal of two-thirds of its troops by the end of 2013, leaving a small contingent to train the Afghan military in 2014.

Glossary

ajala kon   hurry up

Allahu Akbar   God is greater

Amrikai   an American

aram shoo   calm down

azan   call to prayer

baradar   brother

baradar-e bozorg   big brother

barmanu   mythical giant creatures said to live in the caves of the Hindu Kush

bebakhshid   forgive me; sorry

bukhari   heater

burqa   traditional costume, covering a woman's head, face and full body

buzkashi   equestrian sport with a goat carcass

chai   spiced tea

chapan   coat

chapli kebab   minced meat and flour served with nan

haram   forbidden

hich   it's nothing

loonge   turban

jahiliyyah   the old ways that existed before Islam

karakul   sheepskin hat

khwahesh mikonam   you're welcome

khan   the Pashtun title for a village head or a rich, respected person

khoda hafez   goodbye

khoda ra shuker   thank God!

komak   help

korma   a lamb stew with onions, sultanas and spices

Kuchis   Afghanistan's nomadic people

madar   mother

man hoob hastam   I'm fine

mohem nist   no problem

muezzin   prayer caller

Namaaz e Eshaa   the name of the late night prayer

Namaaz e Sohb   the name of the morning prayer

Namaaz e Zohr   the name of the noon prayer

nan   bread

padar   father

perahan toombon   traditional costume of matching shirt and trousers

qabili palao   a dish of baked rice, fried raisins, carrots and nuts

quroot   mint and garlic sauce

raka'at   ritual movement and words during prayer

salaam alaikum   peace be upon you

sug khob   good dog

tashakor   thank you

toshak   mat for sleeping or sitting on

wa alaikum as-salaam   and upon you be peace

wud'u   the cleansing ritual before prayer

Find out more about...

Afghanistan

Behnke, Alison. *Afghanistan in Pictures*, Lerner Publications Company, Minneapolis, 2003

http://www.britannica.com/EBchecked/topic/7798/Afghanistan

http://www.globaleducation.edu.au/2355.html

Conflict in Afghanistan

Chapman, Garry. *Global Hotspots: Afghanistan*, Macmillan Education, South Yarra, 2008

http://www.bbc.co.uk/news/world-south-asia-12024253

http://www.insightonconflict.org/conflicts/afghanistan/conflict-profile/

Children in Afghanistan

Ellis, Deborah. *Kids of Kabul: Living Bravely Through a Never-Ending War*, Groundwood Books, Toronto, 2012

Ellis, Deborah. *Parvana*, Allen & Unwin, NSW, 2002

Grant, Neil. *The Ink Bridge*, Allen & Unwin, NSW, 2012

http://www.unicef.org/infobycountry/afghanistan.html

Child labour

http://www.unicef.org.au/About-Us/What-We-Do/
    Protection.aspx

http://www.theguardian.com/world/2013/aug/03/
    afghanistan-child-suicide-bombers

Explosive detection dogs

Dando-Collins, Stephen. *Caesar the War Dog*, Random
    House, NSW, 2012

http://www.smh.com.au/national/
    barking-mad-bombdogs-have-a-ball-sniffing-out-
    trouble-for-troops-20121119-29m6m.html

http://www.youtube.com/watch?v=ukLSwPYy2bg

Acknowledgements

In several instances I have used material from other sources that should be acknowledged here.

Malalai Farzana, the female politician in *Naveed* who calls herself the Voice of the Voiceless, and broadcasts her message of peace and unity to all Afghans, is clearly inspired by the great Afghan politician Malalai Joya.

I have also used the inspiring words of Malala Yousafzai, the young Pakistani student who survived an assassination attempt by the Taliban, and subsequently addressed the United Nations. I quote her at the very start of the book, and later I place her words in the mouths of both Anoosheh and Naveed.

When Anoosheh is arguing with her cousin Akmed in Chapter 30, she says: 'The power of education frightens the Taliban.'

In Chapter 35, Naveed's thoughts are also couched in Malala's words: *Weakness, fear and hopelessness died. Strength, power and courage were born.*

The opening words of Chapter 35 – *Zemestan khalas shud* – come from Ann Jones's wonderful book *Kabul in Winter: Life Without Peace in Afghanistan*, Picador, New York, 2006.

I used them because they are a cry that Afghans make when the bitter months are over and the hope of spring is in the air. To me that analogy is particularly apt not just for *Naveed* but for so much about Afghanistan.

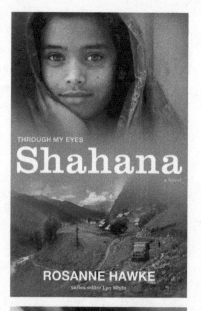
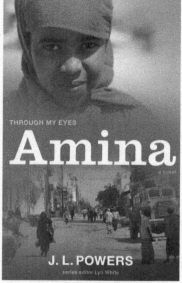
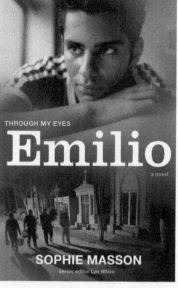